Truth & Mixed Company

I never filled my head up of being the richest person alive, I just want to learn the difference between Los Lagos and Lagos.

- A. C Williams

I would like to thank my family for their patience and support. And also thank those of you who purchased this book. I hope you have enjoyed the short stories.

Table of Contents

Strangers in the Family; The Flip

Brooke Stapleton looked over the crushed box of Dunkin Donuts and reheated coffee in the breakroom. No thanks, the pastries were stale and unappealing looking. She decided to wait until lunch to eat. The corridor was bright with lingering gloom all at once. The sun was still coming up over the horizon when she arrived at work. She looked down at her Citizen watch.

It was a quarter past nine. Locating the tangerine in her bag, she sat alone on the edge of the window and ate it. Never was there a time that she felt confident or comfortable in any environment, even at work. A place where her talents and creativity had a chance to shine. It was like someone knew that Brooke was born to an addict and alcoholic. Was that fact written on her face? Imagined whispers of unworthiness and trash formed into an unseen spirit-like thing that marked all of her steps. Without question, Brooke's relatives' expectations of her were always low. None of their children were Mensa geniuses, but it did not matter.

As it turned out, they went out into the world and did not waste the chance given. She went on to graduate high school, then college. It was acknowledged that she was not an idiot.

They had less to say about her lack of education and became more vocal about my past and present 'sexual partners' real and imagined. Her uncles and aunts were certified slut buckets back in the day, which most people conveniently forget as self-righteousness becomes pervasive in the pursuit of Christianity. Going to church once a month can do that. After you are filled with the holy spirit on Sunday, you can battle hell on Monday.

When Brooke was old enough to move away from them, she did. The best decision for her self-esteem, mental clarity, and soul. Outside of her immediate family, her other relatives were strangers. So, Brooke did not claim to have any family. She was solo and perfectly navigating the life she wanted and who she wanted in it.

The prairie was the land of jobs. Thick-skinned, armed with experience in rejection. She banged on the door of opportunity until it opened.

Her combat boots have a comfortable fit for Dr. Scholl's insoles.

Brooke walked up and down the office corridor. She was still the newbie, so her being the one to get everyone's coffee or retrieval shipped documents kept her busy around lunch most days. Copying documents was a close second. That was how it started, but in a year or two, not how it finished.

She stood outside a cubical with the name BROOKE STAPLETON on its outside. When no one was looking, she took a picture. Speaking of phones, it was time to upgrade, and the iPhone any series was next. Professionals did not have Metro PCS as a carrier. At least, not in her mind. It was not needed like cars racking up tickets in the metropolitan city with excellent public transportation. Yup, an upgrade, she told herself.

During lunch, the ceremonial walks to Panera Bread, she orders the usual sandwich and waits for half the lunch hour. Brooke walked back to the office in ten minutes and paid her last five to wolf down the sandwich and juice. Then, security called up to allow guests in the building, Barry and Bernard. One which was nicknamed Billie, who knew why. It did not make sense that her cousins, dust mites one and two. They were there at the job. Her cousins did not speak much, only when necessary. She disconnected the call after telling him that she was coming down. The nerve, showing up at her place of business.

Dressed in an eggplant blazer and acid wash jeans with black leather loafers are perpetually stuck in the nineties. It was a vibe dressing from that decade, a resurrected trend.

"What is it?" Opting to hear the unwelcome news first—the bitter before the sweet. Why else would they be there? Brooke looked Barry and Billie over from head to toe. Both young men looked like they crawled out of the armpits of Oscar the grouch. The fuck were they doing there, at her job. This is the place where she worked.

"What are you doing here?"

Brooke looked at them and wondered when the last time was, they cut or cleaned their nails.

"And why are you dressed like that? And you smell. Like a weed," she whispered. "What are you doing here?" The first question was asked again of irritation.

"Grandma died. And we knew that this was not news to tell you over the phone. We came down here to tell you this from Harlem. We are busy too. We have jobs too."

"OK, OK," With a mental note she took in the scruffy tennis shoes, jeans, and the sleepy faces. Through the family grapevine, she had heard that they did not work and were a drain on their mother. Brooke did not want to argue with them in the lobby of the building, so she nodded and let him continue.

"It was sudden."

"So, when did she die?"

"She died on Friday."

"Why didn't you tell me Friday?"

"We were so busy, we forgot to tell you. That's why we are telling you today."

"On Monday? Oh, OK, whatever. Are you going down too?"

Brooke was not sure she did not want to go to North Carolina. But for the repast, she had to be there. Then maybe go to the funeral and visit the rest of the family. I had to think about that one. She has not seen those people in a long time. And was better off for it.

"I don't know. Let me call you. I think I might be busy. I may not be able to go down until the funeral. I have to get clearance to get the days off, but I will let you know."

As she turned to walk away. Barry asked for a twenty spot.

"What do you need twenty dollars for?"

"We didn't have any money."

So that was the other reason they came. They didn't care about their grandmother. They never called her. Why are they pretending to be so sad today? And since her aunt, their mother, stole from Grandma Bean while on a drug binge, they were not on good terms.

"We just wanted to come down and ask you for $20 to get back home. It bothers me that you don't answer your phone when we call from Mama's house."

Really, how did they not have any money? They smelled like weed. As soon as the elevator opened the lobby, Brooke looked around, trying not to look at people coming and going on the first floor. A ten-dollar bill was finally located and passed on, exchanging hands. She fumbled around in her pocket.

"Look, that's all I have. Well. Can we have this conversation over the phone tonight?"

"Yeah, yes, sure, sure, sure, because. We just were, you know, dropping through, dropping through." He repeated himself as if he was a parrot. How will you drop in through? It's not easy to find the building. And who in the fuck told them anyway? It was their mother.

"Alright, 'cuz, I'll see you later. It was good seeing you."

"Good seeing you too. And next time, before you come down and quickly visit, call me. I am not too fond of surprises."

Brooke left and walked through the security turnstile and went back up to the privacy of the cubical. It was payday. And she was sure they knew it. She was nearly speaking her thoughts aloud. She squirmed in her chair. And if they were so concerned about grandma, why didn't they tell me she died? Friday night. So, the responsibility fell on her shoulders to make phone calls to find out how and when. And if she was at all needed, take Friday and Monday off to visit North Carolina.

Ten calls it took before hearing the whole story. Mildred Robinson nicknamed Bean did die. After the requested time off was approved, she booked a round-trip ticket to North Carolina. On a budget, Amtrak was the best choice. Tangela at work told her it was the best way to see the country. Why not make it a short trip? She was a one-and-done kind of person. Durham, North Carolina, was not a bucket list destination, but the city was beautiful.

Greetings were awkward. Brooke has not seen most of them since she was knee-high to a bean sprout. Let them tell it.

"Hey, Brooke, where have you been? I haven't seen you in a while." Audrey did not wait for a response but swept her niece up in a gentle hug.

"Well, you know she had suga and that cholesterol." Even armed with that knowledge, her children and sisters still fed her things like collard greens with salted pork, candied yams, and fried chicken.

How could they, she thought? It was irresponsible. Food cooked with lots of salt and sugar can kill people with high blood pressure and diabetes. A simple nutrition class educated her that diseases don't always run in families but recipes and lousy cooking habits. There is an old can with reused lard that flies flew around in the humid shanty house.

A word came to mind. Poverty. Well, Brooke looked down at her watch. "When is the funeral?" The sheepish looks did not escape notice. A blush rose to her perfect shade of the sun-browned face. These people she did not even know yesterday. Brooke spent fifteen years in California and not one phone call, not one happy birthday.

"Well," said the remaining oldest one in her house dress.

"That's why we are so glad you came. I can't find sistas will in a mess in her room, and if I remember, the life insurance policy was only for ten thousand. We paid a few thousand off for the funeral costs." She said and made eye contact with my grandmother's sisters and other grandkids.

"We need some help paying for the funeral." She finished sadly.

"How much was paid?"

"Four Thousand."

Hearing what she feared, she longed to bolt through the door and leave them with their mouths open. They did not even ask me if she could afford this. An embarrassing blush gave way to gritting teeth. These people had the opportunity to ask her to save a trip over the phone.

Aunt Audrey and, sweet old looney aunt Barbara, that woman, she could not hurt a fly. At present, she is in the kitchen cooking and baking as usual. The house that Brooke returned to did not hold any special memories. She never was particularly close to any of them. While her parents were living, half of their salary went to Durham, supporting the elder relatives that raised her mom. Gwen. They were all mahogany brown whereas Gwen was light with green eyes. did not look like any of them. A nagging feeling gnawed at her for years. There was distant cousin Claud, hazel-eyed with a full flat face. Her mother looked like him. Were they even related to her at all? Brooke would look at old photos trying to see herself in the pictures.

"Wait a minute before you say anything," Uncle Walter began. "We can scrape up to seven hundred dollars. All we need is 9,027 dollars." His words brought her to the present.

Brooke just knew it. A Go Fund Me page was about to go up. She could not afford a damn near eleven-thousand-dollar funeral and extra four-hundred-dollar repast. Just because she did not have kids, or a mortgage and a decent job did not mean she did not have any bills. It will have to be a collection taken up or something. Hell, a cremation was only four thousand. Why couldn't they ask for help with that? Brooke had two thousand in her checking and only five thousand in her savings. There was a reason why they did not ask her *before* she came down.

"We will have to figure something out," was the only thing she managed to say. Brooke was stunned and waylaid by her family. They looked to her for all the answers. She had none.

Brooke gathered her things and prepared to leave for the hotel, and only Audrey stopped her.

"Where you are going, baby."

"I made reservations for the Holiday Inn. I need to shower and rest, but I will be back to help sort out the paperwork."

"Why don't you stay the night here? Walter's son John will fix up the couch in the spare room. I know we got a fold-away bed somewhere around here. Sleep here. That way, I can fix you some grits and eggs in the morning. I think I can send somebody to the store for some bacon."

The thought of bacon turned her stomach. Yuck, she thought. Brooke was a vegetarian for a few years. If any of them spoke to her, they would know that, and eating pork would give her diarrhea. The tweed couch looked like it saw better days. She passed on the offer.

"No. My job paid for it. I would hate to turn their gift down"

At the hotel, Brooke ordered room service and showered. She was dog tired but could not sleep until she gave twiddle dee and twiddle dumb a piece of her mind. She was tricked into going to North Carolina, and she did not appreciate being lied to.

"What?" Barry answered when Brooke woke him up to share what she had learned.

"There is possibly no life insurance policy, and nobody down here ain't got no teeth or money. This was a trap. I feel set up. Y'all don't know what I have in the bank. I am finally rebuilding my credit and ultimately saving some money. How much are you and your brother contributing?"

"You know we are not employed, and my mother's disability can't help cuz. Try to be understanding. I don't have any money. Why do you think the family sent you down there?"

"WTF, man? Are you kidding me? Start that Go Fund Me page tonight. Call all relatives, have them contribute, and call me in the morning."

The click of the send button signified that the conversation was over. Once again, she asked how they dared. Brooke wanted to pack and catch the first flight out, but first, she needed sleep. She burrowed down in the four-pillowed queen-sized bed and turned off the television and lights.

In the morning, Brooke Ubered to her grandmother's home. The yellow house needed a power wash. The garden needs to be tended to; the porch swing replaced the inside renovated. As Brooke walked toward the kitchen, she realized that she was the topic of a distasteful conversation.

A man's voice sounded like Uncle Walter's. Unemotional and tactical.

"Who gonna tell her? I'm not. She ain't even family. The house is about to be auctioned. I had to do something. The life insurance is only worth twenty thousand that can cover the expenses for the house stop sale. And Brooke's money can pay off the funeral costs. We have to settle *our* debts. Don't worry about Brooke. She can afford it."

At the mention of her name, the tips of her ears felt hot and probably turned red. Oh, she said to herself. Brooke politely knocked on the door. When she entered, they were smiling, eyes shining. She breezed in with a serene smile plastered to her face. But it was full, a storm was brewing inside.

Audrey pretended to be as sweet as ever. What Brooke mistook for senility; her grandmother's sister was crafty. Brooke was determined to play their game.

"It is a beautiful day out. Did you make those grits that you were telling me about?"

Audrey relaxed and smiled. "Why yes, I did just for you, sweety."

Butter-filled grits in a bowl of salty scrambled eggs minus the bacon.

"You want sugar or cheese on your grits, baby."

"Salt, pepper, and cheese. Your grandma liked sugar on hers. You wouldn't understand. It's a southern thing, you know."

After eating, Brooke piped up and asked to see all the papers to look for the policy. But Audrey and her brother Walter already had the insurance policy down deep in the pocket of his overcoat. "Well, I better move along," Walter said.

"Okay, see you later then," Brooke responded. "You, old coot," she said under her breath.

Brooke worked day and into the night organizing and reorganizing paperwork. This was what she did at work, and she was good at it. Even if her mother was not biologically related to grandma Bean. These people raised her mother, and she vowed to help all she could. Great aunt Audrey and her brother Walter stopped going to school in the fifth and sixth grades to sharecrop however that did not stop them from trying to outsmart her and steal their dead sister's money. At least they thought they could outsmart a college-educated woman, less than half their age. How cute.

They did not understand the will because those dummies did not read it right, and they could not collect on it without alerting the other family members. Lucky for Brooke, the company holding the policy was written everywhere for grandma to remember the name before she died. Her memory was slipping long before she passed away. They all seemed to forget. When relatives stopped coming over it was Brooke's mother sending money.

Brooke remembered that Grandma Bean was neat, but at present, the house was a mess and in disrepair. Her other grandkids did not even help her clean her room. They were useless. How would they know where to look? Upon further investigation, they did not know what all her grandmother had. She had a modest stock portfolio. Brooke called her supervisor, explained the death in the family, and requested two more days off.

Monday morning, Brooke took an Uber to the local insurance company. She showed her driver's license, the funeral director, and the owner was a black man; he was happy to see her and then told her she was the beneficiary of the home and all that her grandmother invested in. It totaled up to one hundred fifty-seven thousand. The house only needed fifteen to be saved. Brooke then asked for fifteen minutes of his time. Signing all necessary papers, she left.

The house was sold, and the funeral cost was covered. Mr. Rawlings was instructed to take care of everything and mail her the rest in a check. She gave him her address, went back to the hotel, and then boarded a train home. Grandma Bean was given a fifteen-thousand-dollar funeral by relatives that had forgotten about her. The repast was catered. It was with the best money Brooke's dead parents could afford. The headstone paid in full, with instructions to inscribe a few words. It read; See you soon, loved ones.

Pembroke Pines was paid, and Medicaid and Medicare papers were turned in by Uncle Walter's children then there was ten thousand dollars for Audrey and Walter. Pembroke Pines was grateful to receive it. The nursing homes would be able to take them in a month or two. The rest of her "kin" could stay with their children.

Mia; Mama's baby. Papa's? Who knows

Zipporah Mia Rubenstein stood in front of a Davids' bridal shop earlier that day. She did not have an excuse for Thomas yet. She returned the emerald-cut two-carat platinum ring, and predictably, he called their parents.

"Mia, why did you say that? Why did you call off the wedding?"

"Mom, I want more."

"What was so hard to believe? Weddings were just fancy parties thrown by people showing off."

Was it a life's goal to be someone's wife? Is it necessary to belong to another person? What does that mean anyway? Mia picked up the golden-red fruit with its leaf still attached to the stem. The farmers' market was busier than usual, so close to the holidays.

Buzzing and squeals from the children weaving through the crowds chasing each other. Was it wrong for her to want a child but not a husband? And the only reason her mother wanted him was that he was a dentist. Protection and comfort are her favorite words. Mia crossed her eyes because she kept saying that.

Her mother was livid. She had been planning their wedding since her daughter and her friend's son were in middle school. It was not arranged, but it took a lot to place them together at the mall, dinner parties, and school dances. Her daughter, regrettably, was one of these new-aged modern women.

There is nothing wrong with living comfortably and being protected from poverty and recession. Trust me. It is not noble to live poor. It is a struggle and a poverty mindset.

Those words again Mia thought of protection and comfort, but she did not mention love in her mother's mind, which will always come later until it doesn't.

Tommie tried to be the tough guy laying down the law with me as if he were setting a precedent with me; if I did not get out, that would have been the actual marriage. And he is not even Italian. He is

Jewish. His name is Thomas Goldberg. "Tommie" is the name he went by with friends, emphasizing the last syllables. He lives in complete fantasy. Pretending to be a wise person and an actual smart guy are two different things.

He had better be careful, or someone will call him on it, like a real gangster, then what. I would have been a widow. No, I made the right decision, she told herself.

"Mom. What if I wanted a child but not marriage?" Mia's mother lowered her voice, squinted her eyes, and hissed. "Do you mean single parent? Sorry but we're not black people. We don't do things that way." Her mother was angry. Mia was mortified. Little did her mother know that Zipporah was the name of Moses' Cushite wife. What would she say if she knew? Mia went from shock to giggling.

The first Zipporah probably looked more like the model Iman than Greta Rosen.

"This is funny to you?" The volume of her mother's voice increased.

Well, that was an incredibly racist comment, mom, her daughter thought. Mia looked around to see if they were overheard.

"Remind me never to take you to my church mom or around the other schoolteachers."

"I am just speaking the truth." She bites out in her Yiddish to English accent.

After escorting her mother home, she returned to her tiny one-bedroom in Williamsburg. It was overpriced. She had a view of the bridge. Mia grabbed her favorite yellow mug with a smiley face. With a hot cup of fragrant Earl Grey tea, she curled up like a kitten on a secondhand tufted navy-blue armchair. Cradling the cup, wondering, could she? Did she dare have a child without a husband? Her culture never deviated from its norms. The best yeshivas and bat mitzvahs have a high-earning professional to marry. Talk about vain pursuits all in the name of protection and comfort. Of course, marriage was preferable to a lawyer or a doctor with a private practice. What was the big deal? Mia wanted to know she was not a lawyer or a doctor who had no aspirations to be.

The newspapers that usually gathered dust and dirt had the most interesting, classified ads one day after work. Mia might take a look. She placed them on the balcony and watered her plants before leaving.

The number 46 bus traveled slowly down the street, heading towards downtown Brooklyn. It was Saturday. It was time for the weekly Farmers Market meet-up; she was not in the mood to see her mother. Mandy and Robin are other schoolteachers from work, they invited her out for Drinks in Manhattan and dinner, but it was 2 pm. No time to change clothes. Plaid shirt and blue jeans. Her blond hair is in a neat low pony.

There was no talk of marriage or babies; however, her age was of sudden interest to Zoya Rubenstein. Thirty-five and still beautiful, but the clock was ticking were the parting words she had for Mia.

The number four train took Mia to lower Manhattan. Outside seating was available. Mandy ordered her usual Cosmo, Robin her sour apple martini, and Mia wine spritzer. She was not much of a drinker. And the thought of taking public transportation alone drunk scared her shitless. The paella and salad she ordered arrived quicker than expected.

Another round of drinks, ladies, it's on me. Mia looked up, looking into beautiful baby blue eyes. A guy at another table with his friends. The rainbow of sexiness. One was a black guy with a bowtie, the other guy Asian and equally handsome. Mandy commented under her breath, that it was the amalgamation of hotness.

"Yup," says Robin.

"Okay," Mia chimed in just one.

"Alright," he said with a wink, it was oozing cheese, but it was okay.

Robin reminded her in her mother-hen voice. "We don't know them, so let's not get drunk. Last drink for the night," she told them, widening eyes to indicate that she was serious. As the only black friend in the group, she was expected to choose the handsome African American friend, but she was skeptical of all three and did not engage much. Mia realized it was assuming right away, she was her mother, she thought. The women stayed reserved even after two drinks.

Mandy, the bold one, asked if they were regulars. What was each person's occupation? One is a dentist, a pharmacist, and sleepy eyes a sales rep for a drug company. Robin wheedled their ages out of them. The men did not want to divulge that they were no longer in their twenties, much like women hesitant to say that no one even checked their identification. How embarrassing to reach an age that no one questioned it? How dare they guess they were all in their thirties correctly. The check came, and the guys offered to pay it, but none of the women drank that much to allow it. The guys' names were Rory, Anton, and Stewart, and apart from the introduction, they were strangers. Numbers were exchanged, Robin called an Uber, and ways parted. Mia stopped her swimming head in her apartment with an ice pack strategically placed on the back of her neck.

She filled her tub with steamy water and poured drops of her expensive rose oil perfume. Thomas gave it to her last year as a Valentine's Day gift. He was thoughtful even when he pretended to be a muscle head. He called while she was having dinner, but she swiped left. Mia wanted someone to talk to about the baby fever slowly groping her. But did not have the luxury of opening up to everybody about it. In truth, she did not want to see disapproving looks or her snide remarks about something she was considering.

Sunday morning a gray dark cloud floated across the sky, yet no rain was forecasted. The phone rang. It was Zoya.

"Yes, mom."

"I called last night at eleven. You did not answer. I was worried."

"Mom, I told you I was going out last night."

"Still check-in, Bubeleh. The city is dangerous at night. Are you coming over for dinner? Your father is at work, so I, you, Yaya, and Agatha, our neighbor."

"No thanks, mom. I am exhausted."

"Do you want your father to bring you food later?"

"Mom, that's not necessary."

Mia's breakfast was simple. She made two boiled eggs and toast for breakfast and remembered that the newspapers were on her balcony. She flipped to the back. That was where the classifieds were.

Artificial semination testing. Now that's a thought she said to herself. She could pick the kind of father she wanted to have for her child down to the looks. The baby could have two white parents or just one. It may take two to three sessions. The kicker was it was ten thousand dollars per session.

"Damn it," she swore. Why was it so expensive just to get pregnant? Maybe she could try a natural way first. She called Thomas.

"Hey Yo, did you drop off the face of the earth? I have been calling you since last week."

"Uhh. Sorry about that. I have been so busy."

"Did you call me to tell me that you have changed your mind?"

"About that, Mia started. I have not changed my mind. I do not want to get married. Can we talk here at my apartment?"

"Sure, I will be over in an hour. I am driving from Great Neck, almost there."

Mia busied herself cleaning up. She was smiling. Why did she not think of this sooner? Thomas loved her. Of course, he would agree. There was no reason why he wouldn't

"An hour later, her doorbell rang, and Thomas leaned on it twice."

"Dollface, let's go out to celebrate"

"Celebrate?"

"I have not seen your pretty face since you called off the engagement in a week."

"We are not engaged, Tommie. I suggested that we wait, that's all."

"Yeah. Right, he answered, deep in thought, shaking his head." Mia was so nervous that she went back and forth, calling her boyfriend, Thomas, and Tommie.

"I can cook at home or order in Chinese perhaps."

"Or I can make reservations at a nice restaurant like Nobu, " he answered.

"But I have something I want to discuss with you, and it is private." She thought that a public restaurant was not the place to talk about him being a sperm donor for her child.

"Is everything all right? " he asked, zeroing in on her belly, smiling."

"Great, and NO, I am not pregnant."

"Oh okay. That would not be a problem for us," he reassured.

"No, Tommie, but that is precisely what I want to talk to you about." He looked confused as Mia pressed on.

"We have been dating for two years, and it has been great."

"Continue.," he smiled. Which annoyed her because she was losing her nerve.

"You would make a great husband and father. The only thing is I am not ready to be someone's wife, but I am ready to be a mother." Thomas's face turned red, and the smile dropped off his face in stunned disbelief.

"Do you have any idea what you are saying to me right now? You do not want to be my wife, but you want my child?" Incredulous, he thought as his voice rose in anger with her weird statement.

"I offered your respectability of being my wife, but you want to be my child's mother. Is this what you picked up at the inner-city school where you teach?"

"I know this is a surprise, but I thought about it. I am not sure that I can spend the rest of my life with a spouse. What if we don't get along? Half of the marriages end in divorce, and I do not want to put my child through that."

"Stop speaking. I feel insulted. This conversation feels dirty. I asked you to marry me," he rationalized pointing with his hand.

"Mia, do you not understand that marriage is a commitment and certainly having a child is the commitment between parents to raise the child properly. I am a man that takes that sort of thing very seriously. That child would be my namesake. How could you ask me that? Do you think that little of me? What did I mean to you? What did I ever do to give you that impression of me? I need to leave now." He asked the questions not expecting an answer. And he headed for the door.

This was not going the way she thought it out in her head.

"Wait. I did not ever mean to insult you. I know you are a decent man, so I asked you. No one needs to know. It can stay between us."

"BUT I WOULD," he exploded. "This doesn't seem right now. I do not know what television show you watched or what baby mother you spoke to down at that school, but I am not continuing this conversation." Thomas slammed out of the door. He was gone and pissed. He did not understand. How could he? Would any upstanding man agree unless he donated his sperm to a clinic?

Her father was furious. It was apparent that Thomas called her parents. Mia was awash with shame and guilt. Her father was dissatisfied with her actions. Her mother was livid.

"How could you say that to him? Are you Meshuggeneh? You hurt his feelings. Apologize now! Today!"

"Mom, I didn't mean to hurt his feelings, but I have been thinking about this for a while."

"I don't care what you think, " she screamed into the phone. 'This will not be happening. You will just marry him and have all the babies you want. You will quit that job and help him at the office, and this conversation never happened. Do you hear me?"

"Yes, mom, I hear you, but no, this is your life. I will figure this out"

"Without our help then," her mother retorted. The call ended. Mia sat on the floor and cried at only one o'clock Sunday afternoon. That spiraled quickly; she thought later that evening. She drank her last cabernet and had a headache. Although she could not explain how she felt, she knew exactly what she wanted. And Mia can admit that it did not make sense, but it made sense to her, and that was all that mattered.

The next day, during her lunch break, Mia stopped by the bank, opened a second savings account, and called it 'Little One.' She made a promise to deposit a portion of her paycheck. On her way out, she saw a familiar face.

"Hello there, Stewart called out. You are even prettier in the daylight." Mia did not notice his flirtatious stare.

She was so distracted that at first, she did not hear him—the handsome Asian guy sitting on the far left of the Pharmacy.

"Hey, how are you?" Mia could not recall his name, although it was only Saturday that she saw him.

"It is Stewart. He held up a hand. It's okay that you did not remember me. Most don't after looking into the blue eyes of Rory or the dark obsidian gaze of Anton." They both laughed. "I am glad they are at work," he then said.

"Are you free Friday night? I know a great Thai restaurant called Dragonfly. Are you free?"

"I am free," she responded. A light-hearted date could make her feel better, but Friday seemed so far away. It was only Monday.

"How about Wednesday?"

"Perfect, looking forward to it."

Mia dodged her mother's calls at home, and Thomas called twice. Her father called to say he was shocked and needed a moment. She did not expect a quasi-liberal older couple to jump on board but try and understand. And give her the benefit of the doubt. She was not crazy. Monday and Tuesday flew by. Wednesday rolled around, and Mia agreed to meet Stewart after work. As promised, they went to the Thai restaurant. It was a while. Mia had curry, so the dinner was fun, and Stewart had a profound sense of humor. She was wondering why he was not married. And so, she asked. She was not prepared for his answer. He was married.

He was separated from his wife. Both are Korean. The marriage was arranged. However, his wife did not want to marry at the time. Both were fresh out of medical school. Both husband and wife working as residents for the same hospital can take a toll on a new young marriage. So, it was over in a year.

"We got an annulment. Our families were devastated, but it had to be done. We were unhappy, and any parent would rather see their child happy alone than married and miserable. She was a great girl, just not my girl."

"Oh," was all Mia could muster to say. Stewart walked her home after the date. When he smiled, his deep dimples peeked out.

"You want to come up for a minute," Mia asked. At the open invitation, he smiled but shook his head. He had an early meeting. "I will call you," he said and was off. Mia replayed the date in her mind. Stewart did not seem to mind that she was just a teacher and was happy there were no pretenses between them. They were themselves.

It was a few days before they spoke again. This time she asked him out on a date. It was a picnic in the park. Over the next few weeks, it was a movie date. A cook-at-home date. Stewart cooked a dish called jajangmyeon.

"The dentist? He cooks too?" Asked Mandy. "I thought for sure you were dating the sales rep with the baby blues. You both could have had little blond cuties, except his eyes are blue and yours are brown."

"Nope. He was also handsome, and Stewart seemed more down to earth, and he was easy to talk to."

"How was he?' Mandy probed.

'So, how was he? If that is what you mean, we did not sleep together, we just met three weeks ago, and Thomas is still calling asking for an explanation."

"About what?"

"Mandy, can I tell you something?"

"Sure anything."

"I want to have a baby, but I do not want to marry."

"Sounds like a big responsibility, a baby is a blessing. This sounds impressive. I wish you luck."

"I am so relieved to hear you say that Mandy. I will be thirty-six later this year. I wanted to have a baby by thirty. At this age, the options are fewer than say years ago. I have considered artificial insemination sessions, but they are expensive. I have been saving up for treatment."

"How much is it?"

"Ten thousand dollars"

"Whoa, that is expensive. Does our health insurance cover any part of the cost?"

"No. it does not, and my parents are furious that I turned down a potential son-in-law for them."

"I can imagine. You did tell me that your mother was planning to marry you off to Thomas since you both were in middle school. And now, her hopes are dashed. Give them time to lick their wounds. They will come around."

Thomas called a month later after the blow-up in the apartment. He called to apologize, but he regrettably stood firm on his principles. Mia said her last goodbye to her childhood friend and boyfriend. Mia softly kissed him, and he turned and left for the last time woefully. It was not as hard as he thought it would be.

Three months passed by, but Mia did not see Stewart much. He scheduled so many appointments and oral surgeries during that time. Mia's father surprised her with a puppy. He was sure that her desire to have a child without a husband would change with a fur baby. It was a passing phase anyway in the sixth month. Mia checked her savings, and she more than reached her goal. She saved 13,750 dollars. It was finally time to make her appointment.

Stewart called and asked to go out Friday night for a double date. Anton and Robin have been secretly dating. And there was a Cuban restaurant in Brooklyn worth checking out.

Soul de Cuba Cafés were painted turquoise blue, and the terra cotta planters' mosaic tiled floors with wrought iron candelabras felt more like a vacation than a place to eat. Robin called Anton a week after we first met and has seen him ever since.

Stewart slowly danced with Mia until closing. He chose the Cuban restaurant so he could dance with Mia. He had been fascinated with her since the first time he saw her, but he was sure that she was interested in Rory as most girls were.

"It would help if you had days off. I know that you are busy."

"Two patients canceled their surgery, and I have the morning off."

"Ohh, Mia smiled. So how about a nightcap?"

"Lead the way," he said with a smile.

"I always wanted dimples. You have a beautiful smile."

"You as well," he responded.

Back at her apartment Mia ran a bath. That morning, she was jogging, and her dry shampoo left her hair limp.

'Do you want anything to drink like some beer or wine or ice cream?' Mia was nervous.

"I rarely eat sweets late at night, but I will have a glass of wine."

"I will be back. Mia sank into the tub, pulling her knees up. She placed her head on her arms as she hugged them. Finally, she thought soon she would be a mom. Her thirty-seventh birthday was only seven weeks away. Mia went into the living room only to find Stewart sleeping. She hated to wake him, so she placed a light blanket around him and went to sleep in her room.

Saturday morning, Mia opened her eyes to breakfast in bed. A single rose coffee and French toast. Mia reached up to hug her guest for his thoughtfulness. She ran to the shower and asked him to join her. Helping him out of his clothes, they made love for the first time. It was glorious. Slow and passionate. Satiated lying in her bed, her head on his chest intertwining hands, he stopped to trace the edges of her full lips. He was more than fascinated. He was becoming infatuated.

With a peck on her nose, he announced he had to leave. He had a scheduled surgery at four, he dressed and promised to call her later. Mia paddled around in house slippers and walked to the living room where she weighed the pros and cons of her choice but ultimately called to schedule her appointment. It was six weeks out, so they were backed up. After the six weeks, it was another four weeks before she could get an appointment.

One morning as Mia prepared for work, she cooked a spinach omelet. The sulfuric smell of the eggs made her run to the bathroom. Mia emptied her empty stomach. She called into school for a sick day. And since she was on speaking terms with her mother again. She made Mia a Matzo ball soup. The broth was light and all she could eat.

Unfortunately, nausea did not subside, and she was beyond lethargic. Was it food poisoning? Was it another illness? Mia scheduled herself a doctor's visit.

Dr. Shmidt was the family practitioner for many years. Her quizzical expression transformed into a smile.

"Congratulations. You are having a baby."

"What?" was all Mia could manage to say.

"I said, " You are pregnant. So, when are you and Thomas having your wedding? I expect my invite in the mail."

"I am no longer seeing him. I am seeing someone else.

Mia was filled with panic, fear, then joy. She questioned her ability to be a good mother, and thoughts about, will she be ready? Will Stewart be angry? Will she have her family's support? Can she do it alone if she had to? So many thoughts.

"What will you do now?"

"Dr. Schmidt, I am going to throw a small party. I am going to celebrate a miracle."

A year later, Mr. & Ms. Stewart Park married. It was in an office at the justice of the peace with her parents in attendance. Ten close friends and family were in attendance, and Lucy slept quietly as her parents finally got married.

Cotton Eyed Joe

At the truck stop, Melanie Nez parked her eighteen-wheeler at the dock. Her mother called. There was another financial catastrophe brewing. Her father's grocery store caught fire, and the insurance company refused to pay for damages. Not to mention the mortgage was two months behind. Her sister's tuition was due, and her husband's hours were cut at the auto planet. She felt like crying. Never did she need a miracle more than right now.

Just then, Michael Gates, another truck driver, pulled in. They had been secretly flirting with one another. It was harmless. Michael was easy to talk to and easy on the eyes. He always said how impressed she was that women were commercial truck drivers and how empowering that must feel. He was an owner-operator that owned three trucks. They made their way to California and Florida weekly. Melanie worked for a private company with a fleet of fifty. She had dental and sick pay. So even when she only made eleven hundred a week after taxes, her children had medical coverage.

Hey, he asked, looking into her face. "Have you been crying?" His Texas drawl was comforting standing at six feet compared to Melanie's five foot six. She had to tilt her head to see him when she stepped out of her cab.

"It's nothing," she answered.

"Doesn't look like it. But I don't want to pry."

"Ever feel like the world is only on your shoulders."

"Yup, I can recall that feeling.

"Well, that is how I feel today."

"Want to talk about it? Over dinner."

"I have to drive back to Pennsylvania in the morning, but I need to clean up first. One of my guys picks up a load and pushes it down to Florida, so I have time if you do?"

She did not want to burden him with her problems. Just then her cellphone buzzed in her hand, it was her husband, Matteo.

He called for her to Western Union money. The bills she had forgotten to pay on her last break.

"Okay, I will send it. Stop yelling. I am under a lot of pressure. And you know full well I only took this job because you wouldn't like it. You did not want to leave the kids with my mom, and you did not want to leave your mom." He yelled a bit more. She lowered the volume so that his yelling would not hurt her ears.

"I am hanging up now. Okay."

'Fucker.' was the only word she could get out. Michael walked over and handed her a napkin and his number when she was ready to use it. His driver stood next to his truck and waited for him handing over a duffel bag.

Melanie stayed at the Super 8 motel only to take a shower. She was able to wash her clothes, detangle and brush out her hair. She braided two long pigtails to dry. Her hair was cold and wet. The heavy hair on her neck and back was a hassle.

Dinner was late, and drinks were flowing. More drinks and problems were dissolving, if only for that night. Melanie sent Matteo three hundred dollars. For all the financial problems they were having, the money barely covered everything. She scheduled to go home in two, but he could not wait.

After a trip to Memphis, she would bobtail home. The ranch-style home on the edge of town was off the reservation. It was the only thing she liked about it, that, and the desert flowers her mother planted. All of the mail would be waiting on the hall table. Melanie remembered that the electric bill was due after she sent Matteo money. She did not bother asking about her husband's pay. She understood that he was doing his best. At dinner, she was distracted.

"If only you worked for me," Michael then said.

"What?" Melanie asked. She had not been paying attention to the conversation all night.

"You seem stressed out, Melanie." Then he motioned for someone to bring them more beer.

"I'm okay." She placed her hand up for him to stop asking for information. "Things always work themselves out."

He did not press but offered a bit of advice. "Problems are easier to deal with when you share them."

That was spoken like a man trying to get laid, she thought but nodded in response. And he added that she should never be afraid to ask for help.

"We, drivers, need to stick together. Well, I have to go. Where will you be tomorrow?"

"I have to drive to Memphis, Tennessee, drop a load, then go home and deal with a few things."

"Think about working with me. I will pay you more than this rat shit company that you are at."

"Okay, I will give it some thought. Goodnight," she shook hands with him. She remembered that she had her driving gloves on and took them to shake hands with him again.

He noticed that her hands were soft, nails slightly chipped but that came with a man's work. Her hair was wavy and black. It was shiny from her washing it. Her dark eyes lowered, she had small white teeth, and her lips slightly parted. They parted ways.

When Michael met back up with his driver. He asked if she was one of theirs?

"No," Michael answered. "But she will be."

Back at home, Melanie went with her mother to the insurance company, it was local, and she only went after a series of calls that went unanswered. They were given the run-around.

Mr. Baker, the customer service rep at the front desk asked if they needed an interpreter.

"Hablo Espanol?" His long-drawn-out vowels sounded like Texan to Melanie. The customer on the landline was put on hold for someone else to answer while he looked over the beauty before him.

"We are not Mexican," Melanie informed him. "We are Native American." The conversation was already starting on the wrong foot.

"Oh wow, how interesting a real live Native American. here sitting in my office,"

He was nervous, surprised, and chuckled. They are not extinct. Was it a long-standing belief? she thought. Melanie looked to her mother Inez who raised her chin to look down her nose at him

'Windtuccum,' she then said. It meant, fool.

"Oh, you're welcome," he said, smiling.

"Uh, what did she say?" He asked Melanie.

"That is hard to translate, but it means close to truly yours."

"Oh wow. That's amazing. Moving right along, I think we can help your father, uh, where is he, by the way?"

"Home recovering from his injuries." But he was pissed about the insurance claim being denied. He stayed home, so he did not lose his temper. It would only make matters worse.

Mr. Vitale, the office manager, promised to give at least half of what the written policy stated. Desperation and fear that it would be rejected wholly stopped Melanie from complaining.

Her mother, Inez, gave a final 'Fuck You' to the insurance rep, but it went over his head again. Her mother, in dramatic fashion, twirled toward Mr. Baker closed her eyes, and said, "Only when the last tree has died, and the last river has been poisoned, and the last fish has been caught will we realize that we cannot eat money." And once again, he was impressed. His eyes were closed and he felt as if he heard a benediction.

"Wow. Uh. Thank you for your wisdom."

In the truck, Melanie turned to her cackling mother. She gaffed as he did in the office.

"We do not have time for this mom."

"What? He deserved it, the crook. Man don't eat by bread alone." And I cussed him so much in my mind I have to go to church tonight. "Will you take me?"

"Sure, I will."

"Will God forgive me?"

"Mom, I believe so."

Her daughter put the old truck in reverse and drove off down the road, that meeting only took care of the store. Melanie called the bank to ask for an extension for the house payment at home. She would pay it off the next paycheck at the same time her sister needed the tuition money paid in a week, or she forfeited her spot for a chance to go to school.

Ingrid refused to stay in Arizona and send Belle to a reservation school. Most of the payments were covered because of a Native scholarship but it was not enough. Melanie and her brother were able to secure a particular loan for native Americans, but money was still tight.

"Dad, I have good and bad news. Which one do you want to hear first?"

"Which one did you want to give me? Remember, I have high blood pressure." Her father giggled.

"What is with you two?" She glanced from parent to parent. "This is serious. Do you want to lose the store?"

"Of course not," he reassured. I am just fed up with being angry about it." What is the agreement for?"

"Half of what the policy is worth."

He sputtered. "Half?"

"Yeah, dad. Half, can you work with that?"

"Damn, crooks." He answered, and the smile was clearly off his face. Just then, Matteo walked in. He smelled of beer.

"Did you pay the light bill?'

"Yeah, I can only pay half. I owed my coworker Steven one hundred."

Only the coworker was Ms. Pat Stevens, and she needed a new outfit.

Melanie blew air. "Just great, Matteo."

She stormed out. The local store was still opened to stock up on food for the truck and food for the house. She turned in time to see a woman with red hair, very fair-skinned staring at her. Melanie looked down at her clothes. Did she button her shirt wrong? When she looked up, the woman walked off, smirking to herself.

In two more days, she would be back on the truck. She has driven to twenty-three states so far. It was a man's job, but more and more women were driving trucks and they supported one another on the road. When she met another woman driver they shared food stories, tips, and personal protection items. She was barely home but she was able to help Matteo pay the bills. her parents were generous enough to do the rest. The only drawback was she was physically exhausted when she came home, and she missed her girls.

There never seems enough time to spend with her family. Melanie's dream was to be an owner-operator like Michael. It was the best decision, better pay flexibility. He set his schedule, made his hours, and tripled her weekly pay.

Wednesday morning, when she left, she kissed her kids and her parents goodbye. Matteo was not at home. He went to work early. Of all the days to leave early. Her black curly wavy hair flapped in the wind as she hoisted into the driver's seat. In the direct manager's office, she was informed that she would be going to Texas, dropping a load, and picking up another.

"Melanie, I'm going to switch your trucks, the one you've been driving needs to be serviced." It was sudden, but she believed it had to be necessary. Why else would he switch her truck?

"Okay, no problem." She surrendered the keys to his awaiting open hand.

"Now, this client is very particular. When you drive the truck in, leave the keys in there. Pick up an entire new load and a new truck. And then move that one to Missouri to another distribution center."

Melanie understood her assignment, but she was baffled about the truck switching. The DM watched her like a hawk before adding how old the trucks were and how they constantly needed repair. He rolled his eyes.

"Of course, not a problem."

She transferred her belongings to the new truck, waited for a sign-off, and got moving. After her pre-trip inspection, everything was normal inside the truck and outside. She drove off.

Melanie rarely went to Texas, but it was a fast-moving town. The warehouses were in the middle of nowhere. She followed the instructions of her DM and was off to clock out and shut down her truck for the night ten hours of driving, twelve hours of rest, and after showering at a truck stop. She walked to the closest restaurant at the rest stop. She had a burger and fries. She climbed into her truck and locked the doors, pressing the kill switch bedding down for the night.

The next day, in the morning, she started going to Missouri. It was also called the show me state. Melanie did not know why, though. But she did know that it was home to one of the longest rivers. If there were tribal lands in Missouri, out of curiosity, Melanie would've gone to them. After the trail of tears, there were no tribes in Missouri.

With a new empty trailer, Melanie returned to her terminal hub for the next assignment.

On long hauls hearing from her family was a cure for her homesickness. Their encouragement was necessary to do the job.

Melanie decided where to stop for the night, it would be Indiana or Ohio. It did not matter. When she called home, her husband was out most of the time, it was frustrating. When they did speak, there was tension.

"Mom, did Mateo come home? I have not spoken with him in two days."

Her mother measured her words. She did not want to tell her daughter. That her husband has not been home. And was seen around town on the arm of another woman. Melanie worked too hard for that type of disappointment.

"No. I haven't he must have conked out on a friend's couch."

"OK, tell him to call me when he gets in. Thank you. Love you too. Bye."

That was strange, she thought. The phone rang again. But it was not Matteo. It was Belle, her sister. She called to say she had two days left. It was either getting the tuition money for school or withdrawing from her classes. Melanie was under pressure due to financial obligations. She decided to look at her savings account to see what she could do. Driving through the night, reaching the outer tips of Ohio. She parked the truck for the night, but she could not sleep. Melanie called Michael. Matteo was out, she did not have anyone else to talk to.

"Hello, Beautiful."

"Hello, Michael, how are you? Is this a good time to talk?"

"It's fine. Where are you now?"

"Just outside of Ohio. And you."

"I am coming from Florida right now. I am on my way to your terminal. Have you thought about working for me? I pay more, and you can spend more time at home with your family."

"I will think about it."

"Sure yeah, think about it, and I will see you in Delaware, Melanie."

Flexibility and more money. It was something to ponder—easy legal money. Melanie Bobtails back to Delaware to her central hub. Michael was there waiting before she got there.

"Hey, Melanie, I'm glad you showed up. I beat you here."

"Yeah, you did," she agreed.

"Are you ready to discuss this? Working with me now. Hey, wait a minute, I said. I will think about it, Michael. I'm not sure yet."

"What is there to think about? I'll pay you more. You could spend more time with your family. What is there to think about is an easy decision."

Upon reaching the depot Michael was there.

"So have you thought about it?"

"Excuse me for a sec, Michael, I will be right back." she wanted to extricate herself from speaking any more about working for him. Melanie went to find her Direct Manager. He was talking to another driver. A driver that started when she did. His back was to her.

"Yep, 1500 to start. That's what I said. Are you ready to start?" His back was towards her, he did not see Melanie's face.

Melanie. said the words fifteen hundred back to herself. She was only making eleven a week after taxes. What the fuck was that? Because she was a woman. And probably because she was a Native American, it could be any reason or all of them. She was getting short-changed again. Melanie walked back to Michael.

"I think I will take that job offer from you. Are there any signing bonuses?"

Michael said, of course. And placed three thousand crisp bills in her hand. Melanie left the keys to the truck. I quit was written on the DMs desk in bold letters.

The routes given to Melanie seemed to zig-zag the country starting from California to Florida. It was hard to follow or understand. Why not use a straight run northwest to southeast. The I-10 highway was better. Strange, she thought while rubbing the tip of her nose.

"Hey, Michael, why are we driving off the Interstate? I-10 would have been the most straightforward way from Florida to California and back?"

He shrugged. It's what our clients want, and we are two or three steps off the I-10, so it's just easier.

"Oh okay. When do we drive out again?"

"Soon," he answered as he placed five thousand in her hands. Melanie made more money than she's ever made as a truck driver. But her husband was still distant. The next time she was home, she decided to speak to him about it. Her sister was able to attend school. Her kids had everything they needed. Her father's store. It was under construction to repair damages.

Something was off. She could feel it. Everything was going her way for once. Bills were paid, and more time at home. But her spirit was not resting. She tossed and turned in her cab while on the road more than she ever has. What was this feeling, she kept asking herself.

Weeks later, while loading her trailer, Reginald asked her to hold a smaller box. It fell sideways, breaking two of them.

"Aww, come on. What the fuck, Reggie? What am I paying you for, and why is she helping you? He pointed to Melanie. She fucking drives, you load."

"Yes. Sir." Reggie was shaken.

"And the cost of that comes out of this week's pay." Reggie looked as if he wanted to challenge Michael on that, but with an odd look and a glance in Melanie's direction, he let it go.

"Michael, it's not a problem. I can help more." Melanie bent down to pick a vase. The dust was all over because it had fractured. The small cloud surrounded Melanie, she started to sneeze. She had a sudden reeling sensation as she stood.

"I am feeling light-headed," she complained.

"Easy now, let me get you some water. Here, sit down."

"I am fine. I just feel dizzy, and my nose is burning."

Michael escorted Melanie to the bathroom and held her hair as she washed her face. Then in an unexpected move. He kissed her on the mouth.

"I have wanted to kiss you ever since we met."

"I am married, Michael, and if we start fooling around, none of the men here will respect me. I will be fair game."

"You are right. I am sorry. Do you accept my apologies?"

"Yes, but don't do it again."

"Melanie, why don't you take the day off, take the blue cab, surprise your family, and bobtail home. Rest up and come back early

Monday morning." It happened so fast that she never questioned what was in the boxes, and then his kiss threw her entirely into a tailspin. He switched up fast hoping it was enough to throw her off. She was swaying as she stood like she smoked something. 'Windtuccum,' the word whispered to her.

But Melanie had no way of knowing the vases were made from cocaine mixed with acetone, baking soda, and the powder food-grade melamine. It is what gave the vases their shape and color. The next few days were spent at home. She was able to take her daughter shopping for new clothes and no hand-me-downs. Her son and father were able to buy new fishing rods. Her husband usually avoided home, but now he is stuck closer to home. Matteo was concerned.

Melanie, he said her name softly like he used to. Melanie stopped washing dishes and gave her husband full attention.

"Yes?"

"You have been working so hard, and I have not been making it any easier. I have been staying out, stressing you out. I have an idea."

"Melanie waited, unsure of what Matteo was saying."

"Let me drive those big trucks instead of you. You can stay home with the kids and rest. You have been driving for years, and I feel less of a man because you have been working so hard."

Her husband was lying, he felt emasculated by his wife. The affair was his way to punish her for being more dependable. Also, if he were being honest with himself, it was because she was more mature, worked harder, and the family knew it. He finally was embarrassed that she could outwork him. And since his co-worker and lover at the factory had become pregnant. She threatened to tell his wife. He did not know what to do about it. The family would hate him, he needed time to think. Matteo did not know how much his wife was making, but if he added all she spent and hid away, it was over three thousand a week. He wanted to take over. He also had a CDL license. He got it months ago. He just never told her.

"Matteo, this is kind of sudden. I like working, and you never wanted to drive trucks before, she added, taking off the rubber gloves."

"Sweetheart, that is precisely why I think we should talk to your boss. We can even alternate every other week. Please. I want to be a better husband to you and a better father for our children."

He was jealous and tired of his wife making more money and his kids asking her for everything.

Melanie did not know her husband's true feelings. He held silent animosity against her, so she sympathized with him. She thought long enough what he said was true. She might have been the reason why he drank and did not work hard enough. His self-esteem needed a boost, and then maybe their marriage would improve.

Her parents watched their children while Matteo and Melanie drove across the country together. Michael did not like it, but Matteo became their backup plan for Melanie. He knew slime when he saw it, and Matteo was as sneaky as they came. When Melanie stayed home with her parents and children, Michael caught Matteo walking around the warehouses where the stone vases were stored. Claiming that he was doing additional post checks gave Michael red flags. So, in a rare move. He sent Matteo to Arizona with three boxes of stone white vases. To his partner Jack.

Not used to staying home off-road, Melanie did not know what to do. She scheduled Parent-teacher meetings to catch up. She visited her sister away at school. She took her children out to dinner. She slept like a baby at night with her new schedule. It seemed like driving was the easier choice. One day while in the grocery store, a pregnant red-headed woman walked straight to her.

"I need to speak to Matteo."

"Oh, hello, I am his wife. Is there anything I can help you with?"

"No. I need to talk to him directly."

Melanie stopped talking. It was her time to stare.

"Is there something you want to tell me?"

"Matteo told me all about you. You are his drug dealing wife that drove back and forth across the country."

"I drive trucks, and what the fuck, did you say to me? I sell…what?" Melanie would have slapped her if she were not pregnant.

"You heard me. He may be working for your old boss, but that is only so that he can live with his new family. I will be giving birth to *our* baby soon."

A small crowd of onlookers stopped to watch as Pat raised her voice. Melanie did not desire to be on a reality Jerry Springer type of show, and the words felt as if the angry pregnant woman punched her hard in the stomach. Pat only talked louder when she was trying to make a scene. Melanie made the choice to not engage her, but she walked out with her pride shredded. Melanie drove home, nearly in tears. So that was his plan. This whiny half-starved very pregnant woman. She realized it too late. They would be stuck taking care of that harpy and her kid.

Melanie sat in the dark in their room for a long time. Her parents took the children to mid-week service. She cleaned up, unable to look at Matteo's things, Melanie cleaned around his clothes and shoes. She touched her bedsheets. They were cold and had been so for an exceptionally long time. As Melanie drove across the country to earn a living for her family, Matteo was sleeping with a co-worker, and now the bitch was pregnant. He made her feel so confident that she approached her at the store. In broad daylight. What was she going to do? She had to wait until he was home on break to ask for a divorce.

During the week, she was anxious. This was unfamiliar territory for them both. Melanie did not know what to say to Matteo. How would he explain? When did he have the opportunity to impregnate that psycho? The following day Melanie moved all of her savings into a private account. Then transferred most of the money from the joint account into her checking. She decided to cry spilled milk later, and who knows if he gave her access to the funds. She checked the deed to the store and the house; they were still in her parents' names. Then she finally called him two days before he came home.

"Hey Matteo, how's everything? Michael treating you right?"

"Yeah, I'm busy. What's up?"

"Where are you?"

"I'm in Arizona."

"That is not our usual route? Since he trusts me and believes that I am a hard worker. Melanie and he gave me a different way which means more money. He never sent you to Arizona, did he?"

"Nope, he never did. I am proud of you, Matteo."

"Sure, you are," he said sarcastically.

"I have a question to ask you. Have you noticed anything strange at any of the warehouses?"

"No. Why?"

"Never mind."

"Are you on the way back?"

"Not yet I am going out for drinks at the ranch out here. So, I will be heading back in the morning. Kiss the kids for me," he directed, then hung up.

Michael was someone she had known for two years. She was confused. He doesn't sell drugs, just…. those vases.

"Wow. I am a fool."

"Reggie and Billy Load'em up. We have a drop to make in the desert," Michael called out.

"Matteo, here have a smoke," Michaels' business partner was friendly, Matteo shrugged and took the pro-offered cigarette. The ranch was a strip club at the edge of Tolleson in Arizona. Although there was a reservation there, Matteo never visited, but he was told that other Native Americans hung out in Tolleson.

Matteo never saw the bartender pour a small substance into his drink. He never noticed men following him to the truck. He barely felt the knife slip in between his ribcage. As Matteo lay dying in the street. He was not coherent as the sticky blood drained from his body. He laid there till morning.

When the call came in from the coroner's office in Arizona, it was to identify his body. Melanie dropped her phone and screamed. Her mother, Inez ran to the kitchen. And heard the terrible news.

Matteo, father of two, loving son-in-law, was dead at forty-two. Since he drove for Michael, he notified Melanie. Michael offered to pay for anything she needed. Traditional burial was held. Matteo was cremated. Pat, his girlfriend, did not find out until afterward. She made a scene at the house in front of the children. She laid down and would not move until police arrived in stunned disbelief.

At the police station, Pat looked and sounded insane. She spun an outlandish tale about smuggling and how the whole thing was a setup. And how his wife had him killed because she, his lover, became pregnant. But Melanie had an alibi. She was seen working at her father's store all day. Pat became ill and hoarse from screaming. She was taken to the hospital to calm down. It was terrible for the baby to be so distressed, the nurses reminded her—the factory sent over Matteo's belongings and his small pension of seven hundred a month.

Melanie owed it to her mother to explain Patricia Albright Steven's accusations. But there was no need. The family quietly moved to California after the house and business were sold. With Melanie's savings, they were able to start again.

Truth & Mixed Company

Red Light Green Light 1,2,3

Holly Mattews snuffed out her cigarette on the bottom of her black shiny pumps, before swinging the door open of the Herald-Star. Robert, her manager wanted to fire her, but he could not. Her work was thorough and respected. Holly was known for hunting down back stories to polarizing newsworthy cases, she helped to keep the paper going. And she knew it.

At present corruption especially in the police department was the horse many politicians rode into their senate or council seats. It was either a staunch supporter of the local police department or clear opposition to police corruption. It was her job to find out the sincerity of those power-hungry phonies this quarter. Pennsylvania was reminiscent of D.C around election time. The bars were jammed with reporters, lobbyists, and of course politicians. And somewhere a story to be reported on. She loved her job.

In a suburb of Pennsylvania in the city of Ardmore, it was quiet as homes barely stirred. The sun had yet to rise but the birds were chirping in Gary Blakes's backyard along with the buzzing of a nightstand alarm. In truth, he needed neither to wake.

Gary's wife of thirty years, Ingrid, had a natural clock. She was up every morning at five. Her routine was a simple one-wake turn on the Keurig machine. Ingrid usually went into the dining room to prepare since she taught at the local high school. If he was running late, she popped her head into their bedroom to wake him. He breathed deeply before getting up, when washing his face in the master bathroom, he brushed his teeth and noticed that it was time to go to the dentist. His teeth were yellowed and in need of a thorough cleaning. It has been a while. In the meantime, he promised himself to ease up on the coffee.

His reflection reminded him that he was a graying fifty-eight-year-old man. Although he stood over six feet one inch, he knew that father time was undefeated. Exercise could help so Gary decided to join Planet fitness on the way home or on his next day off. His stomach had seen better days. He was not getting any younger. He was not grossly overweight like many his age on the job. It was time he went to the gym before it happened to him. He also did not move the way he used to, mainly because of a leg injury. His gait was halting and slower. Thinking of his leg, he bent down to rub the raised zig-zag scar on his knee. He was a walking meteorologist because of his knee, he was able to predict the rain.

"Gary Blake, don't forget your tie," Ingrid called out behind him. The walk-in closet held most of her clothes, and his were hard to find in the swamp of blouses and dresses. It was a miracle that he was able to find anything. His wife handed him a dark blue tie from the drawer near the bedroom.

"Did Ryan call, he asked?"

No. his wife grimaced. "He must be busy," she said and failed to convince her husband.

"Well, as soon as he calls you, tell him to contact me."

Gary has not spoken to his son since he brought home his partner. Ryan waited for a family gathering to tell everyone that he was gay. His lover, Rajee, had a pink lady's scarf around his neck and wore pink studs in both ears. Ingrid was pleasantly surprised that Ryan brought home a guest and had let them in. Her husband stood in the backyard laughing with his brother-in-law cooking at the grill. When Gary walked into the kitchen to hug Ryan, his son turned around while holding Rajee's hand and introduced his parents to his boyfriend.

Beer in hand clattered on the floor while Gary grabbed his son around the neck squeezing. Ingrid was hysterically crying about how dinner was ruined. His sisters-in-law were criticizing him, saying that it was not a big deal. Sure, thought Gary for them it was not. It was not their children who were coming out on Thanksgiving Day. Gary surmised that Rajee was from India, Pakistan, or some friggin place.

The son he raised with baseball, boxing, and good old Irish standards had been sleeping with other men. Everyone was there on Thanksgiving Day, Gary was embarrassed. His parents, Ingrid's parents, her siblings, their spouses, his co-workers, and the fucken neighbors. They all saw, and Gary was not only angry and humiliated. If Gary knew that he was hosting a Dr. Phil type of show at his dinner table, he would have canceled thanksgiving altogether. It has since been over a year. Ryan rarely came home, if at all, and he only spoke to his mother.

Gary adjusted the tie in the mirror, knowing that it was a waste of time to make it look perfect. He hated wearing these things. He knew that it would fall off at some point during the day he used a clip to keep it in place.

The carburetor once again was acting up, so he used his wife's car to drive to work. At his salary, he could not afford to finance a car. He and his wife agreed to double the principal payments to pay off their mortgage early. Gary did not plan to stay on the force for 20 more years. We wanted to retire early to enjoy the rest of his life with his family. He had guessed that doubling the payments for the next five years. He would be able to retire in ten years and live off his pension mortgage-free. He kissed Ingrid and headed out towards downtown Philadelphia.

In the inner city of Philadelphia, sirens sounded in the distance with every far away screech they could close. More police cars arrived. One news wagon and an ambulance did not arrive. They were called ten minutes ago.

"Yellow, her favorite color, was yellow." The babysitter says, crying and another little girl held by either her mother or grandmother was crying and speaking incoherently.

Officer Blake cursed low under his breath before kneeling where the child was. The little girl's eyes were closing. He started yelling, staying awake as if the elevation of his voice had the power to keep the little girl shot alive. Looking at his watch, he wondered why help did not arrive yet.

'Where's that damn ambulance? Why was it taking so long?' This girl could die before it gets here. Stacy Bellamy approaches and offers to hold Kennedy's hand, but the police ask her to stay back. They were playing outside and then all of a sudden. She was scared and didn't know what to do. The babysitter was inside.

"Look at me, don't let go of my hand. Hold on. Stay awake."

The moment she fell asleep, and her breathing slowed; she was at risk of going into cardiac arrest from shock. She was shot in the lower left quadrant of her stomach. The bullet fragments tore through the intestines and stomach. Gary could only imagine her pain. The little with the small voice said that she wouldn't let go. The pressure was applied to the wound, and the ambulance was on its way.

"What is her name?"

"Kennedy."

"Hold on Kennedy"

The ambulance was taking too long.

Kennedy was gasping for air. She needed oxygen fast. The grip on his hand slowly lost pressure. And her breathing was becoming shallow. It slowly stopped. When he checked there were no vital signs. All proof of life ended. Kennedy Johnson was pronounced dead at the scene.

Ernest was declared dead three minutes later while his arms were handcuffed behind his back, surrounded by one plain-clothed officer and three in uniform. Although no officers were harmed and the suspect killed, no one celebrated. life was lost. An innocent seven-year-old child was also killed in the crossfire. The day became night and more people gathered around the yellow tape that surrounded them. The red and blue lights flashed as if the lights alone could speak. It would be shrill and shouting.

It was only eleven hours earlier when Ernest and Kennedy were alive.

"Are you going to the store or not? I gotta cook."

"Yeah, I said I was going."

Ernest put on his jacket running out. His mother spoke to his probation officer about getting him back in school.

Twenty minutes earlier, Ernest had the dice in hand.

"Tag you're it." Two girls squealed and chased each other around a tree on the curb. Across the street, it was a typical day people were drinking and hanging out.

"Seven needs eleven. Let's go." Ernest threw the dice out of his hand against the concrete before he could call a winning hand. A plain-clothed officer rolled up, asking to see everyone's identification. Ernest was on parole, he was not allowed to hang out with his old friends, but he was bored from running errands, so when he saw his boy Daquan, he stopped. Ernest put his hands up and instinctively ran.

"This is an active crime scene. Don't you see the yellow tape here? Do not cross it again."

The sergeant was fed up with the reporters already, and he noticed that two were yet to come. He barked orders at the officers at the scene.

"Secure the crime scene," Gary told the arriving officers.

"Damn vultures They are just doing their jobs, but they were distracting,"

"Did the forensics collect their evidence? Was the mother, Khadejah Johnson, contacted?"

The following week, before a press conference. Community organizers and civil rights activists and a representative from the PBA Councilman Anderson met to discuss the shooting that left a city divided and a community enraged.

"The community organizer Josh Hasselbach and Councilman Wyatt Anderson, Welcome. Please have a seat. I wanted to bring you two men before the press arrives. The lawyers for the family will be making their statements. Josh, would you like to go first?"

"Yes, Ma'am, on the twelfth of May 2004, Kennedy Johnson played outside of her home near Mill Creek Public Housing. At four in the afternoon Officer Blake patrolling saw an ordinance code violation. Young men are drinking in the streets. He goes over to hand out citations or, in this case, for Ernest Nelson, makes an arrest. He was recently out on bail. Ernest evaded on foot through the projects; he stood near Kennedy Johnson playing tag with her friends. Officer Blake yells for him to stop and drop his weapon."

You're it, run, Kennedy, run.

Kennedy, Kennedy. Kennedy!!!

Josh could only imagine the pain, shock, and fear the child felt after the bullet struck her, she was a bystander. The officer was intent on his innocence, but two people were dead. They were living before he was on the scene but now two families were distraught, while he was able to climb into his cop car and drive home safely that night to his family.

"Ernest never discharged his weapon, but Officer Blake did. The ballistics show no gun residue on the now-deceased Mr. Nelson. Aiming for Ernest, the side of the bullet hit a lamp post or streetlight, ricocheted changing the shot's trajectory, hitting Kennedy Johnson in the abdominal cavity. By the time the ambulance arrived, the seven-year-old child was dead on the scene."

"Uhh, I'd like to interrupt here, Mr. Hasselbach. I know that your liberal feelings are invested in this. To make the great officers of this city look unprofessional and dangerous. But the Devil is a liar. I am from these streets, and I choose to clean this area up. If it is the last thing, I do. So why don't you take your fully paid college degree, get a real hobby and join a MET GALA somewhere."

"I resent what you are saying. This is a real job to me, not some hobby. You would rather be a glory hound that unnecessarily took a life than stay on your police force. No protocols were adhered to. Doesn't that concern you? At all."

"At one end of the pogo stick is the scenario that an officer shot a suspect and little girl, or the officer shot a man that killed a little girl. The facts of the case are not lining up, and these officials — including Mr. Wyatt Anderson here in Philadelphia, too busy securing his votes to do a thorough investigation."

"I resent that, also unlike you, I am from here. I have a vested interest in seeing justice."

"Sure you do, and soon if elected you will be vested in Washington to lobbyist where you will be a slave to your political ambitions," Hasselbach noted countered.

"Gentlemen, I am the moderator. Please talk through me. Ms. Vera interrupted their useless squabble. That is why there are lawyers. They are paid to fight it out in court. But this is neither the time nor place."

Mr. Anderson refused to take the rebuff and drop the matter. He had more to say. The truth was subjective to some, but facts are facts to him.

"Ernest shot and killed Kennedy, and Officer Blake did what he was trained by law to do. This city needs law and order. Should we let criminals take over so that children like Kennedy are not able to play outside at all?"

"What a gas lighter," Josh scoffed at The Councilman's explanation of the events that day. He did not believe the Bodycam on Officer Blake was knocked to the ground. After Ernest was shot, five officers rushed in to handcuff him and subdue him. Kennedy Johnson lay dying and unattended until emergency help arrived. Her mother was at work, her babysitter sitting in the house watching a movie.

"Sir, the reports are saying one thing, but your officers are saying quite another. Now lawyers from two families are looking to sue the city. This city is already, excuse the term, bleeding money."

"The facts will be laid out in court. And if you are influencing these families in any way. You might face criminal charges yourself."

"For what?"

"For influencing or tainting, evidence." It took all of Josh's military training not to punch the newly elected council member in the face impulsively. He was the only African American candidate to be backed by the PBA. And he worked extra hard to stay on their good side. He turned around, giving Josh an aggressive look. He picked imaginary dust from the designer overcoat. The following words were said to his opponent simply.

"You know there was a fragment of a bullet embedded in the front bumper of a parked car at this crime scene."

Josh did not believe him.

The officers were grasping at straws, the heat from a "fallen" bodycam, and the death of a little girl put a spotlight on previous complaints against the precinct.

Politics was a dirty game. The people the politicians are there to serve become the casualties. Josh was tired of playing. He wanted to provide answers and accurate solutions.

First thing first. He also had to play dirty by calling in a favor from the news reporter he met a few months ago. Because he could get an interview with a megastar Sable Grant, she was a significant donor to the community center, so Holly owed him one. Josh needed her to start at the police station. Someone there saw something, and they wanted to spill the beans. But could not for the reason of reprisal. There was a code among the officers, like there was a code among the gangsters in the street, no snitching. There was no difference. Only police officers pretended there were. It was just a matter of time.

Kennedy Johnson lived in Philadelphia near Mill Creek housing projects. Her mother worked in a school cafeteria and part-time at a clothing store. She goes to school on Saturdays, taking a phlebotomy class. It was not a perfect situation but not the typical street violence for that community. Activists marched and protested, but Officer Blake was not charged. He was placed at a desk until further review.

No one would talk. They were afraid. The few eyewitnesses contradicted his account, and many were pulled over tags and ran while driving given citations in their homes with a lawyer present.

These were intimidation tactics to scare people into silence. For some, it worked for others. It did not, due to previous harassment.

At home, Gary kicked the covers off. He was unable to not sleep. The little girl dying before the ambulance arrived haunted his dreams. It was a mistake; he knew it was his gun that struck her three days after. Other officers switched the shell casings in the evidence room. If the information were to get out, He was finished. He did not dare to admit the truth even to his wife. It would be like admitting she shot a child trying to rearrest a smart-mouth career criminal. Why did he chase him that day? Ernest smirked and it rubbed him the wrong way.

"Fuck you, Pig." Ernest laughed. It was a trigger, and he would regret it for the rest of his life. Gary was not so broken up over Ernest but the little girl that he held before she died. He did not realize that he was saying Hail Mary and weeping until the ambulance arrived. She was gone but the EMT gave her CPR anyway. She did not make it. The worst part was when her mother came. Her scream was heard long after he showered and lay in bed next to his wife. Ingrid held him, but he cried inconsolably for an hour.

The neighborhood was a powder keg ready to explode by the citizens of Philadelphia. They must learn to meet opposing adversaries with equal force. Not 'burn shit down. Just like Josh had a reporter friend, the officer does as well. Ernest's lengthy criminal history was laid out for consumption in the evening news. Kennedy Johnson's mother was not spared. The year before having her daughter, Khadejah Johnson had a conviction for mail and wire fraud; a check mailed to her in her name from seven thousand was cashed by a friend at a local check cashing place near her home. She knew there was a possibility that it was fake, but she tried anyway. she was struggling, behind all her bills and her rent.

Khadijah cashed the check and they shared it sixty-forty. To avoid jail time, she told her part in the fraud and threw her friend under the bus, but she avoided jail time. First time booked for anything. Ms. Johnson had to pay restitution to the court and do community service for six months. At present, she does not have a felony. However, it put the grieving mother in a negative light. How could that story be turned around? Josh had a few ideas he had to call Holly.

Josh had aspirations of becoming a democratic nominee for the senate. He wanted to get to know his constituents. It did not matter the background. As a community activist, he was laying the groundwork.

Wyatt Anderson wanted the same Senate seat and all the power that came with it. All the city contracts, all the kickbacks protection from the police, and sharing in the payoffs from the mayor. All behind the scenes, of course. It did not matter who drew the first weapon. If they were determined to die, those wild kids would work towards that end, not Community Center nor a community activist will change that.

"Hello." Vera interrupted the two, to introduce herself.

"I am Ms. Vera Farrow, the moderator.'

For the meeting. She Pulled Josh aside and told him to get a conviction. They would need more evidence. Look on the officer's Facebook page, she suggested.

Vera had lived in the community long enough to see the abuse from the officer of that precinct. Rarely were there any convictions or even discipline for the officers' behaviors. That was all the advice she could give to collect all videos from the stores, other homes, and car cams. From around the crime scene. I would start from there, she told Josh.

"I appreciate what you're saying, but Miss Farrow. I am not a detective. I'm just a community activist."

"I understand that, but did you not hear what the Councilman said?"

"He's playing dirty. His police officers are playing dirty. What are you going to do to get a conviction? Because if there is no conviction, there will be blood in the streets and more young people arrested. Community centers damaged, and stores damaged and burned down. What can we do to change that? The press conference began, and the PBA lawyers came out swinging, but the pro bono lawyer Ms. Johnson hired did as well."

At the press conference, with people of the community, other officers, the wife of Officer Blake, and families of the deceased and their lawyers. The mayor had to hold up his hands for quiet.

"Please hold all questions until after both lawyers speak. They cannot say much because it will taint evidence and slay the jurors. This case will not be tried in the media. It had been almost a year, and instead of getting a conviction, Officer Blake was promoted. The investigation has not been concluded."

"The riots in the streets have almost taken it over completely. It would have been avoided if the officer had been fired once the discrepancies were found in his statement. I understand the city would rather kill a criminal than send an officer to jail. However, we are talking about law and order. The law will be constantly violated by those who swore to uphold it."

At Home, Ingrid paced her kitchen floor. Why did this have to happen to my family? She called Ryan to tell him that his father was in trouble, and he needed to come home for them to figure it all out. She reached him at the dorm he picked up at the first ring.

"I don't want to come home, Mom if you have not noticed, Dad does not want me around."

"Ryan. He wants you and needs you at home. He is in trouble. A young man was killed after he fired a gun at your father, and he missed and hit a little girl. Both the suspect and seven-year-old died, and now your father is under investigation. The families are trying to sue the city for millions of dollars. He needs you son. Please come home for a little while."

"Can Rajee come also?"

"Yes, but not right now. Let's wait until this blow over. The lawyer said it would help if we took more family pictures and placed them on the internet."

"Right now, we need you."

Ryan gave in. He hated his father but did not want to see him in prison. He would help them. Then move out of the family home with Rajee.

The activists showed up at the housing projects. Where were they when drugs were being sold there? Councilman Anderson was disgusted the liberal agenda was making his people slaves and complacent. The more the handouts the more they felt entitled. All the officer needed to do was lay low, It would all blow over.

However, Officer Blake did not shy away from the limelight. Some may say he enjoyed it. Family home videos. Police training with the guys. Pictures with his dogs. Probably staged. His social media accounts did not have any personal photos posted until after the shooting. This was free PR. There was more to the story. Holly had to know where to look and who to talk to, Khadejah did want her daughter's killer to get away, and she was sure it was Officer Blake. They were on the same side as what she was hiding. Ernest had to be the one who shot first. Josh may view life with rose-colored lenses, but Holly was a reporter at the Herald for seven years. She had seen enough to know that the inner city had a huge gang and gun problem.

Weeks later after running the story for years the story started to die down. The "peaceful protesting" and later the looting had grabbed the headlines. The media outlets were now overrun with looting and violence instead of their focus being on the tragically killed seven-year-old.

"Hey, Melody." Wyatt was in high spirits when the investigations stalled. The suspect's criminal past was released to the press. And Officer Blake for the most part does not have but two questionable reports against him at the department.

"Wyatt Ms. Holly Matthews has been waiting for an hour to see you. She is from the Herald Press with a few questions."

"Show her in Melody let's not make her wait."

"Thank you, " Holly said as she breezed past the secretary with notepad in hand. A short, bobbed brunette walked in. Hello, My name is Holly Mattews from the Daily Herald, it's a small piece of paper. I am doing an expose on the shooting in the housing projects a few weeks ago. Sorry To bother you Councilmen Anderson I know that you are a busy man. I wanted to ask if you were aware that Officer Blake and Ernest had issues in the past. And that Officer Blake was not scheduled to work near Mill Creek houses that day?"

"Uh. Ms..... uhhhh."

"Call me Holly please."

"As you know I do not make the schedules there at the precinct. How would I have that information? And the suspect was unfortunately a career criminal. I am not surprised that he was arrested more than once. Drugs, weapons, and assault with a weapon."

"Councilman Anderson, his past is not on trial. In fact, Officer Blake had at least two run-ins before the fatal shooting. Doesn't that worry you, that the public will say that cronyism is at work here?"

"Holly, that is not true. I am not personally associated with Officer Blake."

Holly reached in her bag and pulled out an old photo of the Mayor, the District Attorney, himself, and a picture of Officer Blake.

He did not move or change his face as he said oh, what a nice surprise.

"I did not realize a Hero was standing in our midst at the time. If you will excuse me. This picture I have many like them. I did not know the officer, at this time. Holding up two, Wyatt placed them in the air as he said Scout's Honor. Now if you don't mind, I have some things I have to attend to."

He signaled Melody to assist in making the nosy reporter leave.

"I have more questions."

"It seems like you have accusations, Holly. I am a busy man, so I have to cut this meeting short, but we will validate your parking. Have a wonderful day." He stood up with his hand extended to the open door.

"The public has the right to know how the instigation is being overseen."

"That is up to the lawyers and Judge, so please excuse me."

Wyatt nearly closed his office door in her face, he sat down behind his mahogany desk and gently stroked his temples. Holly was annoying. On the intercom he asked Melody to step in and told her to deny entrance to Holly in the future, all other media welcomed.

There were incorrect statements. The crime scene did not provide the full picture. And the babysitter, Latoya, and another little girl named Stacey made statements.

Holly could not do anything anyway. Statements were made on the record. The seven-year-old caught in the crossfire was something altogether different that was a mess. And the Honorable Judge Catherine Gates presiding over the case against the officer was biased, she has family on the force. The lawsuits would be stalled, pushed off for another year, and then dropped altogether. Wyatt took out a small comb and combed his mustache and cleaned his glasses. He was off to another fundraiser. He could not afford to miss.

Mr. Anderson personally placed a call to the mayor's office. That liberal entitled whiny won't get away with this, I assure you that, he informed his secretary. I won't have my career derailed by Nancy Drew and her sidekick, he meant Mr. Hasselbach.

While Mr. Anderson tried the case in the media. The backstory was muddy and unbelievable. Just the way he liked it. He had to stand on the side of the right to look favorable to the voters. In this case, it was the officer, a family-oriented person with over fifteen years on the force, if he was convicted of shooting the suspect in anger or killing a seven-year-old by mistake. It would not look bad for either of them.

"Damn it," Holly shouted, the fucken babysitter. What if she was looking out the window during the chase. But the report failed to mention that Latoya shot at Officer Blake while he was in pursuit of Ernest, the .380 registered to her father. A shell casing from his gun was found at the scene. He had no way of knowing that his daughter's boyfriend was on parole. However, he put a stop to them seeing each other after learning that his daughter wore a gold necklace that was connected to a prior robbery across town. Evidence was crucial. Holly would be remiss if she did not follow up and double-check newfound information.

Where was she now? The baby sister has not left the house since the shooting.

Latoya was preparing for her SATs, but Kennedy was never far away from her mind. She felt guilty but her parents did not want her talking to anyone. The cellphone with the recording of the shooting her mother kept hidden.

At present, Holly knew that officer Blake interned for the current Mayor and the Council member Mr. Anderson was golf buddies. So basically, they all knew one another and had reasons not to spotlight that association. When Josh read the text, he did not know how to proceed, but an angel, maybe Kennedy, sent help his way. Digital forensics and evidence uncovered erased pictures of the mayor and council member before winning his seat. Intern pictures of officer Blake's son with them.

Upon further investigations, Holly learned that officers visited Latoya's family without her lawyer present. Which was unheard of and unethical. But from their point of view. It would be an admission of wrongdoing and lying to the public as paid public servants. If the cellphone recording came out, then Latoya's parents would have to admit that she fired her father's gun at the crime scene. Marking her as a witness and arresting her for unlawful use of a firearm, she was, in fact, seventeen. Her twenty-year-old boyfriend Ernest and Kennedy Johnson were both fatally shot because of it. So, Officer Blake walks. Latoya does not testify because she would implicate herself.

Officer Blake will be named a hero. Kennedy's death will be labeled a tragic accident, both families drop their wrongful death lawsuits, and the city returns to what was. It was a hard pill to swallow. Holly's hands were tied without corroborating or going on record and telling the truth.

It would be a mistake to print anything other than what she was told. The paper could also be sued. And Her journalism days were over. And that was why she avoided Josh's calls while she sat at the bar having a drink. Nothing was easy in this city. She said she sloshed the amber liquor down her throat. It was burning, going down, warming her belly. Josh was leaving the community center. He organized the event to return all unregistered guns. It was a no-questions-asked event. The program director could get three, only three guns off the inner-city streets. It was better than nothing.

Josh went to O'Malley's bar and grill, spotting Holly. So, he said to himself she was dodging his calling. He leaned against the wall unseen and called her again; she picked up her phone and swiped left. She looked wasted. How many drinks did she have? Josh made himself known by offering to buy the next round.

"Hey stranger," he said without making eye contact when he sat down.

"Hey, community do-gooder, " she answered back."

"Where have you been? I have called you so many times. I am hurt. You have been ducking me. Am I a stalker or something?"

"No. You are not."

"What's wrong? Is it something involving the case?"

"I have unwelcome news, Josh. This officer is going to walk. But if a wrongful death is filed against the city, then Ms. Johnson can get some compensation for her daughter's death. To be honest he did not mean to kill Kennedy. He thought he was being fired upon, so he discharged his weapon."

Holly then unburdened herself by telling him everything she knew.

"Damn them," Josh said. What a mess. this was seeming impossible to fix.

"The babysitter was dating Ernest and fired the first shot, she missed but she is the reason the Officer returned fire. She is being coerced into becoming a witness for Officer Blake. Tired of fighting the good fight yet?"

Josh now understood why she was shit-faced at the bar. She felt the way he did.

"Let me drive you home. He took her keys out of her hand. There were no winners except the mayor, officer involved, DA, and Josh bitterly thought of Wyatt Anderson."

"You can't beat the system; you can only try."

"All right, steady," Josh said as he helped off the bar stool. She smelled like honey and whiskey.

The Trial was months away, but Khadejah was anxious. She wanted a conviction and justice for her baby. Latoya's mom called her often because she was a source of strength. On the day of the trial. Past complaints against Officer Blake were suppressed. However, the dead suspect was on trial. Ernest's criminal history was paraded around by the prosecution. The case was tried for three weeks before deliberations.

"Not Guilty."

Khadejah screamed in court Judge Gates demanded that she be quiet or leave.

"He murdered my baby I know it, you know, this court knows it, this damn pig knows it," she screamed.

"Order." Judge Gates banged her gavel and made her final warning. I will have you remove Ms. Johnson. By this time other officers were giving each other high fives. For Khadijah, this was a bitter pill to swallow. Kennedy was all she had. in the world. She had no other children. She fainted and had to be carried out, anyway.

Exonerated!! On the front page in bold letters are the Philadelphia Sonnet, Star News, The Sun, and the Herald Report. It no longer mattered what the truth was; he would not be tried again. Officer Gary Blake was no longer on trial. He asked to be transferred to another precinct, mainly because his coworkers called his son a fairy behind his back. He was also promoted. That bit of news for Holly, Josh, and Ms. Johnson was an insult to injury.

In a twist of fate in west Philadelphia two shooters were robbing a pharmacy high on methamphetamines. Officer Gary Blake was leaving a Philly cheese steak stand he bought two with fries and a Coke. Diet could wait another day. As she crossed the street he was struck by the back end of the evading vehicle. Two cop cars were in hot pursuit. The driver did not see Sargent Blake crossing the street. He was struck and killed at the scene. The driver and his accomplice were charged with vehicular homicide. They were given thirty years each.

Second Class Citizens

"We have a new student. Her family just moved here from London. Her name is Sonali Deepti Jain. Let's welcome her here."

There was a thunder of applause from the group of children seated.

The of Our Lady of Patience. The all-girls preparatory of Gloucester England welcomed their A2 student and then addressed the class. "Let's show how we do it in our town."

Gloucester is the picturesque cathedral port town. And since Sonali's father was a cardiologist, he decided to uproot his family in search of a friendly, slower-paced city. A perfect place to raise his family of four.

Small brown like a light cup of vanilla chai tea with round black eyes, thick straight black hair, and small in stature. But what was lost in stature Sonali made up for in personality. Although she was a rarity there and stood out among the number of black, brown, or others she felt confident about her uniqueness. And, she was careful as the unspoken label, the minority. The few. The bullying did not start right away. First, it was curiosity. and the normal inquisitive questions. Nearly every day she would be asked.

"Where are you from?"

"London."

"No. Where are you *really* from?"

"I was born there."

"But your parents were not. Where are *they* from?"

Over several weeks of settling in as the new girl on the block, Sonali caught the attention of the popular children in school.

"Hand the piece of paper over to Sonali Deepti Jian." Margret Singer was annoyed at the new student in her class. It's not that she was racist, she was the most liberal person she knew. She just did not like the girl. Obediently Sonali did what she was told while her antagonists Betty and Amanda giggled behind their hands. It was

Amanda's idea to call Sonali names and talk about her skin color.

Amanda knew that Sonali was not African or just plain black and she

was not as dark as black people, but she certainly was not white. It was

Amanda, her twin Miranda and her best friend Betty that reminded her

every day. The expression on Mrs. Singer's face did not change when

she read the note.

"Miranda, Amanda, and Betty, I will be calling your mothers

tonight. You are not allowed to pass notes in class." But later Mrs.

Singer felt guilty about having to scold the girls and hugged them in

the hall and gave them the school's important speech. Once again Mrs.

Singer praised the beauty of Amanda and Miranda Todd and told them

to pity the disabled.

When the girls were reseated in class they were smiling.

Amanda mouthed the word 'PAKI,' to Sonali it was an all-

encompassing racial slur reserved for the others.

'Was that it?' Sonali thought. Did she not read the words on

the paper? Her eyes were locked on the door so that the teacher could

at least acknowledge her and make them apologize. Arms tired from keeping them so close to her midsection, shoulders slumped, Sonali waited for the ambulate school bus to take her home. Arriving home, she shared her day with her mother. Mrs. Jain hugged her and simply said to work harder.

"Be the best and outshine those bullies. To them you are different, anyone that does not look like them is different. Focus on your studies and trust me you will do well and make good friends."

Making friends was a little harder than her mother thought. A raised hand in a friendly gesture sometimes did not get the expected result. Sometimes Sonali was ignored.

When she was home alone sitting thinking introspectively Sonali analyzed the hard truth that she was not liked by her classmates. And asked herself if the shoe were on the other foot would she be like them or inclusive? Being a teenager was a vulnerable time in a child's life but being disabled and considered different, a kiss of death, socially. Next to Miranda, her sister, and the popular set she did seem like the odd one out. Would she want to be her friend?

"But Janet's slumber party is this weekend."

"I guess you both will miss it. then."

"Mother this is extreme, three whole weeks"

"That little east Indian girl is annoying. She was pretending to be helpless."

"You can pout and whine, this time I have to set an example. You are Todds do you know what that means in this town? We Todds do not bully disabled girls and be mean to them. Other children look up to you as an example, we cannot let them down. Can we?"

Sonali was not helpless. Amanda just knew it. It was a waste of time to complain to their mother. They were grounded—no outside, no sleepovers, no parties, and on television for three Saturdays. The girls did not mind the tv so much that the parties were another story. Social butterflies with their wings unceremoniously clipped, well for three weeks. Miranda believed that the punishment did not fit the 'crime.' She was determined to get even with Sonali. their mother was disciplining them was unfair. Amanda, her twin of the same mind, planned something for the Easter jubilee involving itching powder. They could hardly contain their excitement as the day drew near.

The following days the twins were quiet which put Sonali in a better mood. At the end of the week, Sonali was in high spirits and her humor drew the other children closer. By the end of the week, Sonali was whizzing down the hall. Cornered the door in her "motor car" doing five miles an hour the door barely was wide enough but if Somali turned her wheelchair fast she could lift off one wheel and take the door at an angle. In her mind, the wheelchair was her motorbike. She was usually the first in class and made it a point to avoid Miranda and Amanda Todd. The twin golden goddess of her level. They started calling Sonali chocolate and usually say. It occurred when she gained more school friends. Classic narcissism disorder Anwar told her at home. "They need help." he diagnosed. Days later it was more aggressive passive aggression.

"Wash off the chocolate on your face."

Some of the children erupted in squeals of laughter. Sonali rolled her eyes, so original were their remarks. Her father, although a doctor did not escape the subtle racism in his line of work. His credentials were checked and rechecked and patients skeptical in the beginning warmed up to him once they saw that he knew what he was doing.

The twins' father was the famous lawyer Simon Todd of the firm Todd & Tolkien. This was important among adults, Sonali noticed. They talked about him with much respect. The teachers outside lavished praise on the family twins for beauty and cleverness. Their mother was fawned over as well. Tall platinum hair color from a box but her diamond wedding rings were beautiful and expensive. And she gestured with them often. Anyone that was on the outs with that family was like a kiss of death because of the social castration.

Mrs. Mara Todd looked fragile to most except when she was speaking. She was poised and measured with her words, she thought before she spoke. It was a great quality to possess. Her daughters were the kind of children other children begged for friendship and inclusion from. But Mrs. Todd understood that her daughters were attention cravers and preferred to make others the butt of jokes than be the target of ridicule.

Sonali hated to be left out, but she certainly did not want to be at the mercy of the girls. Once she watched as Amanda poured milk over Jenny Baker's head for sitting in the wrong seat at lunch. The adults in the room pretended to not see. The Todds held unspoken power in the small town. Vying for favor occupied most of the adults' time in the town.

Later that week Mrs. Singer announced the Easter Spring Jubilee would start during the Easter holiday. The committee of teachers and parents was planned for the evening. And that the hosts for this year were Mr. and Mrs. Todd.

"Yeah," the kids screamed.

Jenny leaned over in her chair.

"They, the Todds, hosted the year before last and had lots of sweets for us. And there were really fun games."

"I might not be able to go," Sonali made an early excuse. She dreaded closed spaces, especially with the twins. The other girl offered reassurance.

"Don't worry about those twins. They are on their best behavior when their parents are around."

"I don't know. I will have to ask."

But asking her mother was not an option. Her mother would only throw her to the wolves. Sonali wanted to skip the whole event. Sonali's older brother Anwar just started University and she would not dare bother him by asking for advice. And he could not be bothered with the travails of his younger kid sister.

Her father called the bullying kid politics, and her mother insisted that Sonali just try harder and get along.

The following day Sonali was greeted by a cool speculative glance from her teacher.

Mrs. Singer feigned concern so well for the little strange girl in her class.

"It has come to my attention that you will not be joining us for the Easter jubilee."

"My mother has to work that day. We won't be able to make it."

"Sorry to hear that," Mrs. Singer replied. But her face did not match the words coming out of her mouth. The funny thing about underestimating a child and their level of understanding, they know when they were not welcomed.

A week before the event Mrs. Mara Todd tumbled down the stairs, or so the rumor was. It was a long-standing belief that Mr. Todd has roaming eyes and a body. It was always easier to ignore a complaining wife than go home. Which led her to the dramatic decisions she made. One particular day after checking the account ledgers, she came across a receipt for diamond hoops that she never received over a month ago. Dinner and hotel reservations. She was parked at home while her husband led a full life with other women.

With determination, a lot could be accomplished. With that solemn thought in mind, Mrs. Todd while walking behind her husband placed her left toe over the right and leaned forward neglecting to grab the banister flying past her husband while three months pregnant. She was at the base of the stairs. At the landing, she grabbed her belly to cradle the cramps and she felt the warm fluid slip from her. She was relieved. He was devastated, he wanted nothing more than a son, but when she discovered his indiscretions, Mara felt this was the best way to punish him. Gaining weight was a sacrifice to bring his children into

117

the world and he did not deserve it. It was a shame that it happened before the Easter Jubilee, she was on the committee. Mr. Todd comforted his wife with a diamond watch.

The first thing the twin's mother did was weigh herself after she returned from the hospital. One hundred and ten pounds. She was almost thirteen. She was growing fat imagine if she went to full term. She did her best to keep her figure and keep up the appearance of happy marriage, doting husband loving, and obedient children. Her Husband attacked with guilt and lavished care and gifts. It made up for times he was away and inattentive in his mind, but it only masked the recurring issues between them. Mrs. Todd underestimated the effect her marriage had on her girls. The girls noticed more than they let on, they knew their mother was unhappy.

Two weeks later the day of the Easter Jubilee arrived, and to Sonali's horror, her mother joined the preparation committee, she would be chaperoning the children at her level. She did not sign up to participate in the play or any of the games. And then there was the question of who would lift her up and down the stage steps. Sitting in her wheelchair watching the decorations go up, and everyone else's excitement Sonali liked being a spectator instead. Her mother talked her into blowing up some balloons as Robert the school janitor taped them high on the walls. He thought the room looked like a sponge cake with too much frosting.

The guests started to arrive in their Sunday best, ankle socks. bright pink or light yellow frocks, sweat suits, jeans bunnies, lamb's balloons, palms everywhere. What was her mother, Mrs. Jain doing? They were not even Christian. Sonali just hoped that her mother's little PR stunt would not backfire later.

The Todds were the last to make an appearance partly due to their mother recovering from a nasty fall. The girls were rushed when they walked through the door, admires and friends flanked them on either side, happy to be in their presence. Sonali placed the break on her chair and then rolled her eyes.

"Exasperating. Their entourage came too."

She would avoid them. Sonali watched them intermittently from afar, Sonali parked her chair near Mrs. Jain. Just then she watched as Amanda searched the crowd, who was she looking for? She was acting suspiciously. As Miranda and Amanda were out of their father's eyesight, they walked in step together with determination.

What are they up to? Sonali followed them across the gym towards the restrooms. They did not see her or hear her electric chair. Once she replaced the break on the chair she sat shocked as she listened to their plan to pour itching power down someone's back. Sonali reversed her chair looking for her mother. But on the way back she parked her chair between too-long coats hanging inside a coat room.

"She will never know I can't wait to see the expression on her toasted face."

"I know right," the other answered.

"We will hide the bag in here and ask her to speak with us, then we'll get her."

"Yeah, I like it, sister."

Their serene smiles were artificial and ghoulish as they left off to find their intended target.

Sonali unlocked her chair and propelled herself forward through the coat to reach the identical coats. Sonali carefully searched their pockets. And found success. The cellophane bag with white powder was inside, Sonali pulled down the identical coats, slowly opened the bag, then proceeded to shake the powder inside the suede pink jackets on the floor. paying special attention to the neck and arm and pockets. When she was finished. The bathroom was the only place she thought of to flush the bag down the drain. Using a stick on the floor she lifted the jackets back on the closet hangers separate from the other coats. Then she rushed out to find Jenny.

The night went well. The play was horrible, the imaginings of a teacher that never fulfilled her wish to be a theater actress. It would have been fine for the children but when Ms. Humphrey took over roles, she could have given to some of her students, that was when it flopped. Amanda slid up to Mrs. Jain and asked where Sonali was when her mother pointed in the direction of Jenny and Sonali at the punch bowl. Amanda all but skipped over.

"Hey, Sonali."

"What do you want? Did you walk all the way over to call me chocolate?"

"No," Amanda stammered. "I want to be friends and my sister agrees that we should bury the hatchet and talk it out. Let's go someplace quiet, like the coatroom."

"I don't want to. I would rather stay in the auditorium and eat hot cross buns." Jenny piped in picking one up.

"We didn't ask you."

"Well. That sounds like a better idea to me." But Miranda joined and they stood behind Sonali's chair and tried pushing.

"Come on," Amanda insisted.

"She said she did not want to go," Jenny intervened. "I am going to get Prefect if you don't stop and leave."

The girls did not push the immovable chair anymore. They were too absorbed with initiating their plans to notice the brake on the wheels.

"Ohhh. All right then. We just wanted to make up."

"Make up for what, you both owe Sonali an apology."

"Apologize?" the girls said in unison. "For what we were just playing a silly prank. Is it our fault that she is too sensitive?" They both walked off in a huff and for the rest of the evening stood next to their father receiving praise for the decoration and catering. By the end of the night, Mrs. Jain suggested that they left early. and called it a night. Sonali was not there when the twins put their jackets on to go home.

A week after the holidays were over both girls came back to school with blotchy red marks on their skin. It was welted from scratching. The itching powder worked to perfection but only on them.

Somalis' thermos held masala tea, her roti and butter chicken were in her Tupperware. She had agreed to share with Jenny who never brought lunch. The school lunch was available but the aromatic smells coming from Sonali's lunch bucket were a pleasant assault on the olfactory. Bangers and mash did not compare. Jenny started out sponging off Sonali's lunch but the more she spoke to her the more they had in common. Both girls were on the outs of the popular set.

The twins with their rash blotchy skin looked warily around hoping no one noticed that under their makeup were the red welts from scratching. someone sprinkled their itching powder, reserved for the little PAKI, all over their clothes. when they found out who was responsible, they were dead.

"Sonali place the naan on the table, darling."

Her wheelchair zipped into the kitchen and then back to the dining room.

"Yes, mom."

She stretched and reached, placing the bread on the table. Mrs. Jain had no intention of treating her daughter like a special needs person. Sonali did laundry, folded, cleaned her room, and helped with the cooking. She had a wicked sense of humor, brave and sweet as a lamb. She was all those things before the accident and still was. If only the other children saw what she saw.

Her mother placed the Paneer Tikka Matka Dum biryani on the table.

"The funniest thing happened at school."

"I was invited to a party."

"Will those snobby twins be there?"

"Uhh, I don't know, but I still want to go."

Secondary school came into session again and halfway through the term, Sonali made friends based on her outgoing personality. Another girl was new to town. Her name was Natasha, she was Irish and Jamaican. Curly sable hair with red flecks brown-skinned and tall. Hair piled up in a ponytail secured with a scrunchie. She had a small nose that tilted upward. freckles on her face. She mostly wore tracksuits and trainers when she was not in uniform. Mrs. Jain was weary as the girls spent time with Sonali in and out of school. Natasha's favorite words were bloody wicked, which tickled Sonali every time, she said it. It was an interesting change from the ice twins.

Amanda and Miranda still wanted to be popular in secondary school and were not above taking their competition down with innuendo, lies, and speculation. Their friends were deathly afraid of what they would say about them if they crossed the dynamic duo. Miranda and Amanda still garnered attention for their looks, bounce light curls, and light blue eyes.

However, that all changed when a girl named Natasha moved into town and the school. The big bad yardie that moved to the small English town. The people of color in the town were 0.2 percent Sonali and her family included. Most people of color were all in London.

Natasha was like a dream come true for Sonali, the young Black girl with the colorful accent accompanying colorful speech made Sonali stick out less. There was a new shiny object around. Now Sonali was included, and unfortunately, Natasha was too. This only pissed off beautiful vain twins with a taste for nasty, pranks.

Natasha had a chill personality and the students got on with her very well. Even the twins warmed up to her, they started hanging out together after school. When invited along Sonali declined, she did not trust the blond-headed duo. And it was good thinking. Natasha was arrested for shoplifting on their outing.

The sales associate was already watching the Black girl and following her in the store with the nick knacks. The alarm went off when Jenny, Amanda, Natasha, and Miranda were leaving. The saleslady searched the girls' bags. In Natasha's backpack were lipsticks, jewelry boxes, and inlaid pearl combs. Miranda talked her into taking them and then pretended to not know her afterward. Natasha was expelled and given a stern warning from the magistrate. It humiliated her grandmother. There were so few Black people, and she did not want her granddaughter to be known as a thief.

Natasha was transferred to a state school. She hated it. But she never forgot the experience, or the way Miranda laughed and walked off while she was detained and her bag searched.

"See you at school. And all Pakis steal. They can't be trusted."

Natasha vowed to thoroughly kick her ass on campus. when she explained what happened. Her grandmother simply said.

"You were set up. The girls tricked you and filled their pockets. You were the distraction. Relax, I will ask to see the CCTV and if they do not give it to me, I will sue them."

This only made Natasha angry. She was embarrassed and still expelled. They made her look like a stereotype and that was the real problem. After reviewing the CCTV, charges were dropped. But the twins were not arrested or expelled. Natasha's grandmother was so angry.

The matter should have been resolved but their father just made it all go away. and gave Natasha's grandmother 'please be quiet money.' Rules are more fluid when people had money and could afford good lawyers.

Sonali and Jenny were the only two girls in the whole school that spoke to Natasha after the transfer. The children in her new school smoked weed in the halls and told the teachers off.

"The work is madd easy," Natasha would say. And she scored an A on all her tests, if possible, she was even more popular than before. Public schools and state schools did not have the same curriculum.

"I am still very angry about the way you were treated, Natasha."

"It is okay. That school was too expensive. My grandmother was struggling to pay it monthly."

"My parents are struggling to pay it now. I thought I was the only one," Jenny shrugged.

"Let's stay friends and call to check up."

"Sonali, we have the weekends if we can. Let us go to the mall."

"Anywhere those blasted twins are not," Jenny added.

Simon Todd was indulgent with his only two children. The boy he wanted dying in utero.

So he spoiled his girls and vowed to always use his firm to help them.

Soon they would be off to university. By that time, the girls would wind down and get more serious. He hoped that they would follow him and become a lawyer but neither had the inclination.

One Year Later…….

Amanda Todd escaped the shadow of her twin sister by joining various clubs at University, Miranda however became withdrawn over time and then angry. It was the separation anxiety that most twins felt when their identity was wrapped in their twin. Miranda thought pretty was no longer the outgoing twin. She was no longer a part of the dynamic duo that she was in primary and secondary school. She was solo. Miranda needed Amanda to feel validated. The terrific Todds were not the same without both of them. Miranda knew her sister's

Achilles heel like their mother. She had a fear of gaining weight and

losing control of her eating habits. It was ridiculous. Amanda was

naturally thin. They inherited that as well as the blond hair and blue

eyes from their mother. It was inherited lunacy.

One day in study hall as Amanda sat near an east-facing

window the sun streamed in, it was noon and the sun was high in the

sky. Her blond curls glowed like cornsilk. He smiled mesmerizing

those that sat nearest to her. She was a flower and her friend's bees.

Her water blue eyes met him briefly. an electric jolt traveled down

their body, and before he knew it he was standing in front of her.

"Hi."

"Hello"

"I am Liam Benning."

"I am Amanda Todd."

Before he could say anything else a figure walked by him, she was

identical to the girl before him. The only difference was that the other girl had a hard edge around her eyes and mouth as if she held a perpetual scowl.

"Miranda."

"Amanda."

"Don't you have class somewhere?"

"Why is that your concern?"

The bickering was inevitable between them.

Liam was confused, he heard that twins were inseparable, these sisters looked like they did not like each other. The hostility between them was apparent. It was like watching someone argue in the mirror.

Liam was dressed in a cardigan loosely tied around his shoulders. Worn leather loafers. He did not have a clear idea of what path in life he wanted to take. Amanda would talk about their dad so much everyone knew he was a lawyer with a law office on the west side of town. But she was clear to add that she had no intention of also becoming a lawyer. She was interested in social work. What a laugh Miranda had when they were alone during Christmas break.

"Amanda, you need a counselor of some sort. How could *you* be one?" Miranda was at her best when she was cruel.

"You never seem to change Miranda. I see why you are so popular. Oh. that's me, not you." Amanda countered.

"Liam prefers me, and you're just upset about it."

"Wrong sister. He is just as self-absorbed as you. Thank you for taking him off my hands."

Miranda settled into the sofa of the family room, annoyed she was out of response. She took out her cell phone and ordered a dozen of Amanda's favorite donuts.

"I would like to order a dozen caramel coconut crunch with extra clotted cream."

She left the box on her sister's bed with an apologetic note.

Amanda, I hate it when we fight. I got your favorite to say I am sorry.

Love U,

Miranda.

P.S Don't eat them all at once.

Amanda snatched them from her bed to throw them in the trash. But she wanted only to smell the freshly baked goods. She felt "cured enough" to do so. As she opened the box Amanda decided to lick the toasted coconut off one. And then put the rest under her bed.

After many canceled dates by phone. Liam became uninterested. Amanda kept missing his call after the first-time meeting Liam. He did not know if it was intentional or just plain forgetful, but it hurt his pride. He wanted to get to know the vibrant Amanda, but princess Miranda clearly did not approve. She was always there watching and waiting. It was hard to have a conversation but that was not the problem. Miranda was coveting.

She fell in love with Liam and all of the attention given to Amanda was not reciprocated. His affection was wasted, and Amanda was not interested. Jealousy was something Miranda never experienced before. But there she was jealous of her twin. As a young woman, she was used to getting her way. It was not normal to be ignored. And it stung her pride to be the second choice.

Miranda visited her sister regularly and joined the clubs Amanda did, which she did not care for. Nature preserves, saving the planet, chess, event planning committee. Amanda found kindred spirits at those meetings. Not a shopping club, not a wealthy girls club. She changed from the time they were children and to Amanda's disappointment, Miranda did not change at all. She was childish and mean-spirited.

Liam and Miranda ran in the same circles, so it was only natural to see him. The coincidences became more often, so much so that they started to date. Amanda was surprised but not much. The cupcakes and candy bars her sister sent her weekly would stop. It was hard for someone who battled every day to maintain a healthy relationship with food and did not need the temptation. Bulimia was something she battled with on and off, especially during times of stress.

Liam and Miranda dated for a year before nuptials were exchanged and it was before law school. She sacrificed a huge wedding and relocated to Cambridge for Liam to finish his studies. as long as he was happy. They could be happy.

After five years of marriage, Liam Benning was dead. Miranda was beside herself with grief. She was hoping to be married all of her life like her mother. Liam, the first and only man she had ever loved was gone. Dead at twenty-six. The day of his disappearance started like a normal day. Up by five protein shake out by six light jog for five miles. At seven in the morning, he returned, took a shower, Spinach, and egg whites, and out by eight on the way to the office nine. Monday to Friday and occasionally Saturday.

The officers took statements from the housekeepers and Mrs. Todd-Benning. Liam was fished out of the River Severn fully clothed. Amanda held hands with a distraught Miranda when she heard the news. Miranda fainted and needed to be placed in bed due to the stress.

Several days before Miranda started the search party after Liam disappeared. It was over a week that he dropped off the face of the earth. No one at the office had seen him. Miranda was beside herself with worry. She soothed herself while shopping. When he finally came home, he would finally want to stay and repair their marriage or so she told anyone who asked. Her behavior was increasingly strange. But grief affected everyone differently, people argued. It was the belief that Miranda was just keeping herself busy. And her father was concerned. It was weeks before the body floated up to the surface. Liam's foot was caught between rocks in the reverse undercurrent. When the water slowed his foot dislodged. Liam's now bloated body was free.

Their heads rocked back after the car violently started. A serene look plastered the woman's face while her husband looked in askance. Liam Benning's quizzical look did not stop Miranda from driving her breakneck speed.

"Hold on, slow down. My father gave me this car."

"Correction, he gave us this car. As a wedding present, remember."

He blew air out in exasperation. It was his car, and she damn well knew.

"Am I driving too fast?" Her eyes raked his slim frame. It had been years or days since they made love. His work kept getting in the way. Miranda defied her mother and her father to marry him. And after four years of marriage, her obsession with her husband only grew. His attraction for her was waning. He had achieved what he wanted. Liam worked for his father-in-law in a big firm earning the most whether he took a case or not. Thankfully, his father-in-law had no sons. His mother-in-law miscarried something to that effect before he married their eldest daughter. Only older by minutes. A replica of her was born moments later. The car jolted after Miranda released the accelerator pedal in their vintage two-seater Mercedes Benz.

"Hey, babe, watch the car."

The rumors of Liam cheating finally reached her ears, again, and she could no longer ignore the late-night meetings or the perfume lingering on her husband's clothes. He was so dismissive of her accusations she started to doubt herself. It was the worst feeling to challenge yourself. It was akin to not trusting yourself or losing your mind. She was too fabulous to go crazy slowly. So, Miranda did what any curious wife would do. She went digging for the truth. Liam liked that his wife was paranoid about him. It was an emotional payback for neglecting him when he needed her most. He failed the bar examination. He almost quit, but he would inherit a law firm when his old father-in-law retired. That was the only push he needed.

"Who is she this time, Liam?"

"What the bloody hell are you talking about?"

"The girl? The woman? the man?"

"You are just insulting me, love. I would never play hide the sausage with a man. And I am utterly faithful to you, my dear. You are just paranoid. You need to schedule a visit to a doctor or have someone come to the home. Love, you are the only one for me."

He is lying, Miranda thought and continued to drive at breakneck speeds. She was not her mother. She would not just look the other way.

"Miranda, come on. Let's enjoy the ride." Liam's nervous laugh bubbled up as he looked at his wife, driving like a madwoman. She had no way to know that he was sleeping with his new intern. It started very innocently but all his affairs did.

"Sweet piece of ass, Natasha." A mail clerk joked in the breakroom.

Liam reminded his employees that sexual harassment is prohibited in the workplace. He did not feel comfortable with his employees discussing her in that way.

After getting to know her at work, he could no longer reduce her to a piece of ass.

It all started innocently enough. The longer he knew her the more he saw the hidden qualities that men found attractive. Liam drove his new paralegal home one day because her car was in the shop. And that was how it began. She mentioned Liam's wife because of the photo on his desk.

"I am guessing that the pretty blond is your wife?"

"Yes, it is."

"She looks very familiar."

"Her name is Miranda. She was born and grew up here. I take it you're from London. It is more culturally diverse there. Right?"

"Actually, I was born in Ireland. My mother is Irish and my father Jamaican."

"You have quite an interesting pedigree. If you don't mind me, saying."

"Not all. Out of all the things people can say, that was one of the nicest."

After he dropped her off and after Liam went home. He thought about her twinkling dark eyes. Miranda was waiting up. As they made love that night Liam turned her around, closed his eyes, and thought about their beautiful face, long fluffy frizzy hair, and dark twinkling eyes. The differences between them were beyond physical though both women were beautiful. Both Miranda and Natasha were operating on different sides of the spectrum as far as looks and personality. Whatever it was about Natasha drew Liam like a bee to honey.

Natasha could not believe that she was working for Miranda Todd's husband, she was sure he had no clue how she was. She massaged her shoulders and planned to go for her morning run. It was the only way to keep in shape without paying a monthly fee. First, she called Sonali whom she spoke with regularly. She still lived at home.

Natasha offered the spare room but her mother wanted to keep her close. It was funny that they both worked in law offices.

Sonali picked up after the second ring

"Wassup Natasha."

"You will never guess who drove me home tonight."

"Who?"

"Miranda Todd- Benning's husband."

"As in married? Husband?"

"Yep."

"I work at her father's firm; trust me I did not plan that."

"She was such a trash bag when we were kids."

"Well. She and her sister were awful."

"Does she look the same?"

"Unfortunately, pretty slim."

"Is her husband attractive?"

"Yes. He is but he is my boss and some lines should not be crossed."

"So, how is it? That he drove you home?"

"My motors in the shop."

"Likely story."

Natasha laughed and Sonali said what she was thinking. "You are utterly wicked. I am hanging up now."

Because of cases and late-night talks after work, Liam found out that they were marathon trainers. It made it possible to sneak time with his new interest. Natasha jogged every morning at seven. Miranda would not get out of bed to turn off the television. She refused to join her husband in jogging in the rain.

She invited him in for tea which he graciously accepted. It was tea and lentil patties. She brought them to work. She would bring lunch for Liam or share it with him during their lunch hour.

Natasha was vegan and a great cook. She was the complete opposite of his wife. Liam liked that. Where Miranda was fairly light with blond curls. Natasha was deep cocoa brown with deep-set black eyes and lashes. Where Miranda was gracefully thin. Natasha was ample in waist and breast. Where Miranda was dry, sarcastic, cold, and jealous. Natasha was free, warm, and caring. It was only supposed to be an occasional fling, but he liked her increasingly as time went on. She was comforting like an old favorite sweater.

"Liam, are you listening?"

"Sorry?"

"The fundraiser is next weekend. Mom and dad are going. It is expected that we will be there too. We will need to order your Tuxedo and my outfit too."

"Sure, plan the whole thing. I trust your style."

As Miranda spoke, he was thinking about Natasha. He never meant to fall in love with anyone other than his wife. He was curious like other white men that came in contact with different beautiful women of color. She was just his little exotic plaything; she had become more out of nowhere. Her accent was refreshing, other than the stodgy long vowels of his homeland. She was colorful and enthusiastic about life. His wife's idea of passion was changing the day for intimate play.

Liam was fitted for his tuxedo, and Miranda was splendid in her emerald, green silk dress. It was a compliment against her pale skin. Liam kissed her bare should you look fabulous. A golden clutch bag in the shape of a shell was worth the five thousand dollars Miranda paid.

The sun crept up over the horizon. It was the first time Liam had stayed out all night. Natasha lay next to him. He watched as light, and shadow played across the room. Her wild oily hair was draped over a satin pillow. Golden light caught her shoulder. Her skin glowed amber, the sandalwood mixed with rose oil that she oiled her skin and hair. She smelled warm and spicy. Liam did not think about the lie he would tell Miranda. He thought about how he could wake Natasha and make love to her again. She turned in her sleep, opened her dark hypnotizing eyes, smiled, and said good morning. It was official he was in deep with her. But not enough to leave his life of comfort after all the whole idea of marrying Miranda.

It was afternoon by the time when Liam stopped by the office. His father-in-law was sitting at his desk waiting for him.

"I had a grueling day and crashed…" Liam trailed off once he saw his father-in-law's face.

But Simon held up one hand, cutting off any reply.

"End it now. I gave you this position, and I can take it away."

"End wha… I don't know what you are speaking of sir."

"I believe you do. End it now, before you lose everything. You are my son-in-law and employee, but Miranda is my daughter."

With that, Mr. Todd walked to the door and then down the hall to his own office. Miranda walked into her husband's office. No sooner than her father left, Miranda walked in. Her back was stiff. Her eyes looked like they were crying. Liam walked over, hugged her, and apologized for making her worried. He was at the office all night. Miranda looked at him but feigned ignorance. She had the keys and the alarm passcode to all the law offices and buildings her father owned. Liam was not at the office, and he did not come home.

"My husband works so hard. Grabbing his chin. I am proud of you. I was worried, but it's clear that you were busy working for dad."

Liam could tell that she was not fooled.

"Go home first. I have a few things to do, but I will be there shortly." In a surprising move obediently, Miranda headed towards the door. Her father met her in the lobby and apologized for forcing Liam to work late.

"He must have gotten tired and slept in the office on the roll away."

They teamed up and lied to her. She fumed that her husband lied, and her father covered for him what was wrong with this picture.

Later that night, Miranda made all of Liam's favorite biscuits with potatoes, peas, and onions with sangria. And tomato jam on the side. She added a teaspoon of salt to the tomato jam and three tablespoons of cayenne pepper to the biscuit and potatoes. She even added horseradish and sangria olive juice.

She set the table as she usually would, lit candles, put fresh cut flowers on the table, and filled the drink glasses.

Liam walked in at six on the dot. He was early. He did not want to disappoint his wife. She was a great woman outside of her coldness, selfishness, and classist behavior. In truth, he was lucky to be married to her. She could have chosen anyone to fall in love with. Liam bought her roses, although they had a garden filled with them. White fragrant rose. She greeted him with a soft, slow kiss.

"Wash up, she said. I gave Judy the night off."

"Oh, okay, swell."

The table was perfect, and Winnie, their Labrador yelping around outside the garden. The dining room in muted light romantic was a word.

Miranda made her plate, and he sat down for the meal after coming home. She is dressed in a sexy black tight dress. Her waif figure looked so delicate and frail. But fragility was not a word suitable for Miranda or her twin Amanda.

Miranda placed the meat and steamed vegetables on her husband's plate.

"I cooked the beef with red wine and herbs. I hope you like it."

Liam took his knife, cut a generous portion, and greedily stuffed his mouth. He was so grateful that she had forgiven him for staying out that he was pleased and surprised when she offered to cook. She rarely did. The heat in his mouth was not felt right away, but he was so hungry that he chewed quickly and swallowed the meat almost whole. The peppers gave him a delayed kick of heat in the back of his throat. He reached for his Sangria in a panic to discover the bitter, salty taste. Liam reached for his glass of water. It was vinegar. Sputtering in pain, he ran to the kitchen, looking for bread or milk. He had to settle for water from the kitchen sink. He was sputtering in outrage.

"What the fuck is wrong with you, Miranda?"

"Where were you last time? You were not at the office."

"I was working for your father. Ask him, okay. You ruined a meal."

"No. You did that all by yourself."

"Miranda, seek professional help. Before your delusions and paranoia tear us apart."

And after his final statement, he grabbed his coat to leave, only for Miranda to wrap her hands around his waist and beg him not to. But Liam was not swayed.

"Miranda," … he began before he could ask for a separation. Miranda kissed him while rubbing her body against him. Anger gave way to desire as they stood in the grand foyer and ripped their clothes off. He grabbed her hand and pulled her towards the stairs, but they never made it to the bedroom. Liam was angry. She slapped Miranda and entwined his fingers in her hair and pulled. He grappled with his wife until they fell on their marble steps. Cold hard steps bit into her shoulder. They were spread, held on the ground for half an hour, half-clothed in ripped attire, breathing heavily.

Liam was ashamed he could not look at his wife. Miranda was oddly giddy that her husband still wanted her. As he helped her to stand, he considered starting over with her. Or he could try to find out what attracted them in the first place. But he knew. It was a marriage of convenience for him, but love at first sight for her. Both situations had to be managed or broken. Reaching the bedroom, he contemplated telling her about his last affair and apologizing. But if she could calmly ruin dinner of beef brisket which took hours to cook, she could do more, making him nervous.

The office was having a party. There was always an office party. But it was Christmas. Both Natasha and Miranda would be there. He wanted to stay home. He would make up an excuse and call it off. The son-in-law of the owner could not 'call it off. And it would only look suspicious of Miranda.

The following Monday. Liam asked Natasha to skip the Christmas party for a party of their own. He lied to get her to stay home.

"Natasha. Why don't we have our own party?"

"I want to go to this one, " she stood on tippy toes to brush his lips. I have been looking forward to it. This will be our first party."

"But there is a special gift I want to give you. Don't want anyone to see us, babe"

"Okay, then make it sparkly because I am disappointed."

If Natasha was being honest with herself, it only made sense that she stayed home. Miranda would be there. It was tempting to finally pay back the person that had her arrested and ostracized, sleeping with Liam was not enough and backfiring slowly. She missed him when they were apart.

Liam had no intention of leaving Miranda's side at the party. He would just have to make it up with an expensive sparkly gift. The week went smoothly, and the plans put forth by his wife were stunning. The trees in the lobby as well as the Christmas tree on the office floor looked beautiful. It was a shame that Natasha had to miss it. He rang his favorite jeweler and ordered a diamond halo sapphire necklace and small diamond studs to match.

A trip to the tailor the day before, and a cater on the day of the party left Miranda reeling. Amanda should be here, Miranda told herself. How long did it take to cure bulimia? Their mother had it and she was. Their mother died of Cancer, not starvation. This was Amanda's way of letting Miranda shoulder the responsibility of her father's office. She was so selfish to claim mental illness now. Bulimia was just an eating disorder. Miranda rolled her eyes Amanda was ridiculous. When Miranda needed her so much. She was overwhelmed and hiring just the right event planner and food service was important a lot was expected of a Todd party.

Later that night, Miranda dreamed that she was driving and arguing with Liam. She stirred throughout the night. When she woke up. Her body felt bruised. Her scalp ached, and she had dark circles under her eyes. Volunteering was something she hated but it was a chance to see the less fortunate at least that was why her mother went. Todd & Tolkien sponsored a children's home and food pantry, they were all about keeping up the appearances, after all, it was expected of them.

She would be late arriving at the Catholic charity house. She did not want to volunteer, but she did in honor of her mother. Most families were druggies and second-class citizens in Britain on work visas. Some were barely employed, but what Miranda gathered from them was poverty in that part of Europe, and poverty in other countries held two different meanings. Mainly it was people wanting weekly groceries for their families.

One day she found a familiar face in the crowd. It was Sonali still in her wheelchair. She looked different. She became pretty, she looked confident unlike when they were children.

They met eyes. Sonali was the first to turn away, wheeling herself in another direction.

"Wait. Wait," she called. Miranda was out of breath. "Wow, those chairs are similar to little race cars. Right."

The electric wheelchairs were not that fast, she was exaggerating. She must be uncomfortable, Sonali thought.

"Remember me?" Miranda still glowed with health. Her curls bobbed, and her eyes were still ocean blue. But her sneer was gone.

How could Sonali forget someone who made secondary school a nightmare?

"I am fine. And you."

"I am so sorry to see you in a place like this. Here I will get you two bags of food. I will be returning." Miranda rushed off, happy to be of some use and no less to an old-school chum. The unfortunate thing. Miranda thought she knew that Sonali would have a hard time in life because she was disabled. She wouldn't be able to take care of herself properly. She would always need someone to take care of her because she couldn't walk. It was good that Miranda was there to help her that day.

"Wait," Sonali called behind her, but Miranda was off showing charity to the less fortunate. And the poor dear was still in the chair. So unfortunate, well though Miranda, it was her Christian duty to help the poor lady.

"Miranda," Sonali called,

"I am coming, my dear, wait. Just then, Miranda returned with two crates of food, one with meat and grains, the other with vegetables, and two burly men were there to help her.

"There you are sweetheart. That will be enough for you and your family." Miranda's eyes were bright, finally happy to be of service in a natural way.

"Miranda, you did not have to go through the trouble."

"No Problem dearie, I will ring a car to fetch you Luv."

"Miranda. I am not here to get food."

"Are you not in need of services?"

"No. I am not."

"Then why are you here?" Miranda huffed. She was baffled. Why else would her old quadratic schoolmate be there?

"I am an immigration solicitor. Volunteering my services here. I meet with potential clients if they need my help."

It took a minute for the information to register.

"You are here to do what again. Luv?"

The realization dawned on her, Sonali was a lawyer, an immigration lawyer. Miranda quit law school when she found out she could just be the wife of a lawyer. And after her father passed on, the law firm would belong to her husband, and his many properties would belong to her. Why would she need to work? Why would she want to? She had nail appointments, hair appointments, Pilates, shopping, and spa days, and oversaw the house cleaners when they would slack off. And when she did not watch them clean her home, she was volunteering, her least favorite but a part of her schedule. Miranda did not have the time to hold a job after her busy schedule.

Sonali handed over a card in gold lettering that read.

Solicitor Sonali Deepti Jain

Legal Analyst and Immigration Law.

Rated #1 in the Country

Sonali smiled as Miranda read the list of endorsements under her name. The jealousy that spread over Miranda's face made Sonali smile even broader.

"I have to push off, my brother Anwar is picking me up in five minutes."

"Ohh, yes of course."

Miranda still did not know what to say. She was dumbfounded. As Miranda learned, Sonali's body did not function normally, but her mind was competent.

"Good seeing you again, Miranda."

And Sonali maneuvered into the shiny black car and was off.

Miranda replied after Sonali left.

"She's a lawyer now. Really."

Once again, that thing called curiosity made Miranda turn on the computer and then ran Sonali's name through the database to see if she was a lawyer. Miranda was disappointed with the turn of events. She instead thought that Sonali would be destitute somewhere, unable to take care of herself. She was disappointed that she did not need assistance, but she was one of the top lawyers in the area. As a woman that comforted herself with the thought, she was so much better off than most. This information was a blow to Miranda's pride. Her nemesis survived in life, doing well. 'Oh bugger,' she thought.

Amanda would have bought her building where her law office was and evicted Sonali from it.

Miranda went home, her mood soured by someone else's good news. She slammed the door on the way out of the church office and slammed the door entering her home. She snapped at the cook and the housekeeper. She sat down in front of her mirror and looked at her beautiful blond hair face and smiled.

"At least I am still more beautiful than she will ever be."

It was her consolation prize, and she will take that. Since Amanda was not there, why not dig into Sonali. It could be easy. After all, Miranda was her father's secretary for years.

Miranda found out the law office belonged to Anwar Jain. He owned the building. Damn it, she swore. Miranda decided to call to make an offer only to find out several days later Anwar was Sonali's brother. She could afford to take a few pro bono cases.

During this time Harrison, a private P.I started following Liam Benning at the behest of his wife. It was easy to take the job she was offering five thousand pounds for two weeks' worth of work. His office rent was due, and he would find a way to extend it another week. The first week. He watched the office, nothing suspicious there. Miranda was suspicious and wanted her husband's time accounted for or Liam was working so much over time. Miranda called her father to complain. Father would make Liam behave.

"I'll call him," her father was not convinced that it would work talking to his son-in-law. Delegating Liam's duties to other partners might make him see reason.

But Liam was falling in love with his assistant. It was happening slowly but with every argument, or manipulation by Miranda, his feelings grew stronger for Natasha. The problem was, that he was not sure she felt the same.

It was a Thursday and another late-night work session with Natasha. she was on top of him across the walnut desk in his office after their second climax did, he tell her that he loved her. Unfortunately, at the same time, the detective snapped the incriminating photo.

Liam had scheduled a jog in the morning across town, then gym then home work he had a routine. The only time he deviated from it was when. He was with her. Harrison caught the lovely photo but did not know who to give it to. He would end up selling the picture to Mr. Benning who had the most to lose. After eight in the evening for the first week, Harrison went home and drank a stout and had some chips. It was the second week that any real work began.

Harrison followed Liam keeping a distance. He was sleeping with his intern. Her name was something exotic. Her name is Natasha. Harrison smiled at the thought of Liam getting his kink off behind his prissy wife's back. If he played his cards right, his office would make it to the end of the year.

Miranda did pay him up front, but Harrison called to speak with Mr. Benning to see if he would make a better offer for the photos.

"Mr. Benning, call on line one."

Liam placed down the exhausting stack of invoices to be sure all clients were billed correctly before handing them over to Natasha for processing.

"Hello. This is Liam Benning. How may I help you? Mr. Harrison. You are outside. Yes, I have a minute to come into the office. I will meet you in the lobby."

A man that Liam never met before walked directly to him and slipped a yellow envelope into his hand.

"I think you should view these in private."

"What are these?" Liam opens up the envelope only to close them again. It was pictures of him and Natasha, adulterous ones. Miranda would divorce him, and his father-in-law would destroy his career. Miranda's father had a long reach. And with people vying for Todd's influence Liam would easily be replaced.

"How can I help you.?'

"The question is how we can help each other. I am sure you will produce something." Mr. Harrison slipped his card into Liam's pocket.

Liam called Harrison later that week. The price of his silence was twenty-five thousand. And he agreed to pay it, it was an expensive way to end an affair but the financial ruin of divorcing his wife made it a deal.

It was a shame. Natasha would just have to understand. He would transfer her to work under another partner or give her references to work somewhere else. Either way, it had to end. To her credit, Natasha was very understanding and amiable, but Liam was almost hurt. But she reassured him that it was morally wrong and wanted to end things cleanly. It was better that way. However, Miranda did not hear from the detective. She went by the office in time to see the cash handed off by her husband.

Miranda gained access through the fire escape attached to the building, she crossed the rooftop and opened the back window of Mr. Harrison's office. The nights were out. And the only light available was streaming in from an outside neon sign. Using a metal nail file, she pried his locked file cabinet open. It took twenty minutes. There were no pictures, only a box of negatives. It took an additional fifteen minutes to collect most of them and place the others back.

The following day. Miranda visited a photoshop in a neighboring town. and had them developed? Miranda was enraged, not just jealous. Her husband must have paid him off. Harrison was avoiding her calls. Miranda went home and shredded the disgusting pictures. She did not want to see them again. But it was too late. Her husband being straddled on his desk was etched in her mind.

Weeks later, Miranda decided that it was time to stop by Liam's office to see the bitch up close.

During his lunch hour, she breezed into her husband's office after checking her appearance in the mirror. She spritzed perfume and looked around only to see Liam without a front desk secretary. And his assistant was an older gentleman.

'Hello, Miranda? What are you doing here?' He enveloped her in a tight hug.

'I came…. I came to see you.' Her head swiveled back and forth, searching.

"Are you looking for something?'

"Uhh No. Would you like to go to lunch with me?"

"Sure. I would love to babe. Let me grab my jacket."

Walking out hand in hand. It was odd there were times Liam was inattentive. Touching her hair, and holding hands were all things Miranda initiated. In the lobby, Miranda wanted to do one final check, because the woman in the photos was not there.

"Oh Bloody hell, she exclaimed. I forgot to tell my father about a new client. Get the car Liam it will only take me a second."

"Oh alright, Luv."

Miranda reached the fifteen floor and scanned the office. She passed by her father's office peeking into different conference rooms. She did not see any young girls there. It was mostly older men that worked in the law office. a few temporary workers and older women that worked there for years. On the way out, she realized that it was a waste of time. She felt foolish and walked into the elevator. as the doors closed,

she caught a glimpse of a familiar face. her head was thrown back to laugh at a joke a colleague was telling her.

"Natasha? That was an old school friend."

During lunch Miranda was antsy. She ate too fast and hastened her husband along to get home. She felt sick, and it was not indigestion, as she looked down at a half-shredded photo.

There was her husband and Natasha.

When did they meet and how long was it going on? These were all questions only those two would know. And that slut would only deny it.

"What should I do? I cannot give up on him. I invested too much. I cannot tell my father." Miranda paced back and forth for an hour. Should she ask her husband about his mistress? No. she would not much like her mother, some decisions needed final recourse, with that in mind. She sat at her desk and took out flyers for the Christmas office party invitations.

Natasha held the prescription for Ambien in her hand while Sonali held the recorder in the corner of the warehouse.

"This was great catching up with old school chum," Miranda said with a smirk. "But I have to be off. Things to do." She pivoted her black heels aiming for the door, she heard an odd sound like an elevated bike grating against its chains. But out of the shadow of the room came Sonali Deepti Jain. The solicitor?

"What? Do you ladies want?" and she stressed that word ladies loosely. "What do you ladies require of me?"

"Nothing but the truth," Sonali replied firmly.

"This is all extremely dramatic. Why are we here, don't you think meeting in a warehouse is illegal?"

"Did you kill Liam?" Natasha cut in.

"What on earth are you talking about? Of course, I did not kill him. He was my husband."

"He was sleeping around, that is the motive," Sonali said, pointing to Natasha blocking Miranda from leaving. "Answer the question."

"I did not kill Liam. I am looking for his killer too. How do I know Natasha didn't kill him? Unlike you, I have many things to do. Let me pass. And Natasha, do not bother coming to work. Your employment at Todd & Tolkien is hereby terminated. I will need your badge and access to the file cabinet." Miranda said with a raised chin and then an outstretched hand.

"Screw your file cabinet. Did you kill him? Why didn't you just divorce him? Are you crazy or something?"

"So you or my sister have him. No fucking way."

That was as good a confession as any for Sonali but Natasha saw Miranda's weakness and pressed forward.

"Liam did tell me that he was dating Amanda first. And he liked her better."

"Liar. He loved me and told me so. daily"

"On the days he was not with me," Natasha jeered.

"I would never lose to you, fifthly, foreigners. Go back to where you belong. Leave my country." Miranda's face was red, she was sweating and cornered, she thought she was careful. The plan was well thought out. Executed perfectly, how did these bitches find out?

"There it is, there is the old Miranda Todd we all know and love. How did you get away with it all this time? And we were born here. Please stop pretending to be the grieving wife. How pathetic. I have the traces of Ambien and the flask that he had. I bought it for him because he liked my grandfather's old one. On the day Liam fell into the river there was no way that he would have not swam to save himself. So, I went to your home and stole it. The maid kindly let me take some important files from the office at your home."

"That sounds like trespassing. I will have to let the authorities know Natasha. What will they say when a black woman slips into the home of her dead lover while the wife is out. It does not sound like innocence to me."

"Who cares what it sounds like to you. It had traces of Ambien in it along with alcohol. You are caught. You weirdo."

Sonali glided her chair forward.

"She found the flask, Miranda. When your clothes were wet. You told anyone that would listen to the office party that you were helping me dress. Miranda, you used me as an alibi, I made a statement to the authorities that I did not see you that night or any day after. We are not schoolmates, really you were half of a team of bullies to me."

Miranda ran to the door of the warehouse, but the authorities were outside positioned to arrest her. Unable to accept Liam's cheating she did sedate and drowned her husband, but she was never going to give details.

The investigation was thorough. She did not confess to killing her husband but there was too much evidence to point anywhere else. Sonali and Natasha looked at one another.

"We need a detective agency. We solved this case for them. Why did she have to kill him?"

"Pride. She was a classic narcissist."

"Did you love him?"

"Almost."

"Well. We need a ticker tape parade through downtown," Sonali answered. "She is a real nutter, that one."

The police officer handcuffed Miranda and led her to the police car.

"Miranda Todd-Benning, you are under arrest for the murder of Liam Benning."

Mr. Todd's car screeched to a halt.

"What the bloody hell is going on here. Release my daughter. I mean NOW." He demanded his anger in full force shouted. "Y'know full well my daughter would never do this"

He then turned his fury on Natasha.

"It was that half-caste black bitch. You were fucking him behind my daughter's back, and he was going to leave you. He told me so and that the gimp was always jealous of my daughter since coming here."

"Whoa. Oy' Language. This is unnecessary Mr. Todd please step aside. Let us do our job, we will keep you aware of what is going on first, Miranda will have to be processed."

"Processed? You mean arrested?" His voice rang an octave higher on the word arrested as he stood in disbelief. This is a farce, he thought. His daughter? Impossible.

"I will sue this town, the police station. I will sue all of you."

Miranda's father black shiny sedan sped off behind the police car to have his daughter released after she was 'processed.'

The next morning Miranda was released pending further investigation. She failed her polygraph test. Her father declared it was because of her sensitive nerves. There was a forensic test done on the flask. Her DNA as well as her husband's were on it. Natasha as well as Sonali made a prior statement. The tape from the office party showed the absence of husband and wife. And the CCTV on the docks showed her going to a boat with Liam and then leaving the dock without him. She could not explain why. Miranda was the last to see him alive that night. Without going to trial. Her father persuaded her to take the plea deal offered, which she did. She admitted to drugging Liam with her sleep medication and lowering each limb before tipping him into the water. Miranda Todd-Benning was convicted and sentenced, she received fifteen years in the H. M correctional facility.

The case was closed with mixed reactions to the verdict. Business partners were embarrassed, and associates of the Todd family refused to accept the evidence. Anyone that believed Miranda killed her husband kept their opinions to themselves. It took several weeks but the quiet small town returned. The reporters and sensation of the murder died down and Gloucester was the idyllic place visitors and residents fell in love with again. It was not a big city but a cathedral town where the crime rate still was low even after the dock murder.

What a night Mrs. Jain thought, Miranda Todd a murderer. What was harder to believe was that her daughter that was bullied by her solved the case. The Todds had a loyal following in the town but as the case got underway, the facts were released. And they will have to accept it. Miranda killed her husband over an affair. She stole Liam from her twin sister, Amanda. Then after he had the affair with Natasha, his office manager Miranda killed him.

Mrs. Jain looked at Sonali, her daughter who did not look tired by the news in the wheelchair. She looked energized.

"Don't get any ideas. You are a lawyer."

"From now on, who knows mom. I could open up a detective agency."

"No. I am serious; it is too dangerous. Miranda even crazed is milder than what's out there. My fearless girl, you have court in the morning. Remember Ms. Abdullah was granted her working Visa. You will have to file those on her behalf. And come home early I will make your favorites."

"I can't mom, I have an engagement. I am meeting with Jenny and a few girls from my old school. But I want to say thank you for raising me the way you have. Even anchored to this chair. I feel invincible empowered by your strength."

"Deepti are you getting sappy?"

"No Mom. just stating the facts."

"Goodnight love."

"Goodnight, by the way, how does The Deepti Detective Agency sound?"

"Terrible."

Her mother closed the door. Sonali already knew that Anwar was dating someone at his hospital. Even when his mother already found a wife. They will have to break the news slowly. A fragile waif in the outpatient caught his eye and his heart. She was reading "Shadow Work vs Mirror Work," by Matthew Gold. It was a book he gave to his sister, Sonali. He was a firm believer of all self-help books himself. It helped his anxiety when first starting Med school. Meeting his new friend was one of the benefits of working at the hospital. Anwar would have to tell his mother that he fell in love with a patient. Her name was Amanda.

The End.

Truth & Mixed Company